VIKING

230601763

The Everyman Wodehouse

P. G. WODEHOUSE

The Swoop!
Or, How Clarence Saved England

&

The Military Invasion
of America

EVERYMAN

Published by Everyman's Library
Northburgh House
10 Northburgh Street
London EC1V 0AT

The Swoop! first published by Alston Rivers Limited, London, 1909
The Military Invasion of America first published in *Vanity Fair*, New York,
July–August 1915
Published by Everyman's Library, 2013

Typography by Peter B. Willberg

ISBN 978-1-84159-190-2

A CIP catalogue record for this book is available from the British Library

Distributed by Random House (UK) Ltd.,
20 Vauxhall Bridge Road, London SW1V 2SA

Typeset by AccComputing, Wincanton, Somerset
Printed and bound in Germany
by GGP Media GmbH, Pössneck

GENERAL CONTENTS

The Swoop!

A Tale of the Great Invasion

CONTENTS

It may be thought by some that in the pages which follow I have painted in too lurid colours the horrors of a foreign invasion of England. Realism in art, it may be argued, can be carried too far. I prefer to think that the majority of my readers will acquit me of a desire to be unduly sensational. It is necessary that England should be roused to a sense of her peril, and only by setting down without flinching the probable results of an invasion can this be done. This story, I may mention, has been written and published purely from a feeling of patriotism and duty. Mr Alston Rivers' sensitive soul will be jarred to its foundations if it is a financial success. So will mine. But in a time of national danger we feel that the risk must be taken. After all, at the worst, it is a small sacrifice to make for our country.

P. G. WODEHOUSE
THE BOMB-PROOF SHELTER,
LONDON, W.

Part I. The Invaders

1 AN ENGLISH BOY'S HOME

August the First, 19—.

Clarence Chugwater looked around him with a frown, and gritted his teeth.

'England – my England!' he moaned.

Clarence was a sturdy lad of some fourteen summers. He was neatly, but not gaudily, dressed in a flat-brimmed hat, a coloured handkerchief, a flannel shirt, a bunch of ribbons, a haversack, football shorts, brown boots, a whistle, and a hockey-stick. He was, in fact, one of General Baden-Powell's Boy Scouts.

Scan him closely. Do not dismiss him with a passing glance; for you are looking at the Boy of Destiny, at Clarence Mac-Andrew Chugwater, who saved England.

Today those features are familiar to all. Everyone has seen the Chugwater Column in Aldwych, the equestrian statue in Chugwater Road (formerly Piccadilly), and the picture-postcards in the stationers' windows. That bulging forehead, distended with useful information; that massive chin; those eyes, gleaming behind their spectacles; that *tout ensemble*; that *je ne sais quoi*.

In a word, Clarence!

He could do everything that the Boy Scout must learn to do. He could low like a bull. He could gurgle like a wood-pigeon. He could imitate the cry of the turnip in order to deceive rabbits. He could smile and whistle simultaneously in accordance with Rule 8 (and only those who have tried this know how difficult it is). He could spoor, fell trees, tell the character from the boot-sole, and fling the squaler. He did all these things well, but what he was really best at was flinging the squaler.

Clarence, on this sultry August afternoon, was tensely occupied tracking the family cat across the dining-room carpet by its foot-prints. Glancing up for a moment, he caught sight of the other members of the family.

'England, my England!' he moaned.

It was indeed a sight to extract tears of blood from any Boy Scout. The table had been moved back against the wall, and in the cleared space Mr Chugwater, whose duty it was to have set an example to his children, was playing diabolo. Beside him,

engrossed in cup-and-ball, was his wife. Reggie Chugwater, the eldest son, the heir, the hope of the house, was reading the cricket news in an early edition of the evening paper. Horace, his brother, was playing pop-in-taw with his sister Grace and Grace's *fiancé*, Ralph Peabody. Alice, the other Miss Chugwater, was mending a Badminton racquet.

Not a single member of that family was practising with the rifle, or drilling, or learning to make bandages.

Clarence groaned.

'If you can't play without snorting like that, my boy,' said Mr Chugwater, a little irritably, 'you must find some other game. You made me jump just as I was going to beat my record.'

'Talking of records,' said Reggie, 'Fry's on his way to his eighth successive century. If he goes on like this, Lancashire will win the championship.'

'I thought he was playing for Somerset,' said Horace.

'That was a fortnight ago. You ought to keep up to date in an important subject like cricket.'

Once more Clarence snorted bitterly.

'I'm sure you ought not to be down on the floor, Clarence,' said Mrs Chugwater anxiously. 'It is so draughty, and you have evidently got a nasty cold. *Must* you lie on the floor?'

'I am spooring,' said Clarence with simple dignity.

'But I'm sure you can spoor better sitting on a chair with a nice book.'

'*I* think the kid's sickening for something,' put in Horace critically. 'He's deuced roopy. What's up, Clarry?'

'I was thinking,' said Clarence, 'of my country – of England.'

'What's the matter with England?'

'*She's* all right,' murmured Ralph Peabody.

'My fallen country!' sighed Clarence, a not unmanly tear bedewing the glasses of his spectacles. 'My fallen, stricken country!'

'That kid,' said Reggie, laying down his paper, 'is talking right through his hat. My dear old son, are you aware that England has never been so strong all round as she is now? Do you *ever* read the papers? Don't you know that we've got the Ashes and the Golf Championship, and the Wibbley-wob Championship,

'Paper, General?'

and the Spiropole, Spillikins, Puff-Feather, and Animal Grab Championships? Has it come to your notice that our croquet pair beat America last Thursday by eight hoops? Did you happen to hear that we won the Hop-skip-and-jump at the last Olympic Games? You've been out in the woods, old sport.'

Clarence's heart was too full for words. He rose in silence, and quitted the room.

'Got the pip or something!' said Reggie. 'Rum kid! I say, Hirst's bowling well! Five for twenty-three so far!'

Clarence wandered moodily out of the house. The Chugwaters lived in a desirable villa residence, which Mr Chugwater had built in Essex. It was a typical Englishman's Home. Its name was Nasturtium Villa.

As Clarence walked down the road, the excited voice of a newspaper-boy came to him. Presently the boy turned the corner, shouting, 'Ker-lapse of Surrey! Sensational bowling at the Oval!'

He stopped on seeing Clarence.

'Paper, General?'

Clarence shook his head. Then he uttered a startled exclamation, for his eye had fallen on the poster.

It ran as follows: –

SURREY
DOING
BADLY
GERMAN ARMY LANDS
IN ENGLAND

Clarence flung the boy a halfpenny, tore a paper from his grasp, and scanned it eagerly. There was nothing to interest him in the body of the journal, but he found what he was looking for in the stop-press space. 'Stop press news,' said the paper. 'Fry not out, 104. Surrey 147 for 8. A German army landed in Essex this afternoon. Loamshire Handicap: Spring Chicken, 1; Salome, 2; Yip-i-addy, 3. Seven ran.'

Essex! Then at any moment the foe might be at their doors; more, inside their doors. With a passionate cry, Clarence tore back to the house.

He entered the dining-room with the speed of a highly-trained Marathon winner, just in time once more to prevent Mr Chugwater lowering his record.

'The Germans!' shouted Clarence. 'We are invaded!'

This time Mr Chugwater was really annoyed.

'If I have told you once about your detestable habit of shouting in the house, Clarence, I have told you a hundred times. If you cannot be a Boy Scout quietly, you must stop being one altogether. I had got up to six that time.'

'But, father—'

'Silence! You will go to bed this minute; and I shall consider the question whether you are to have any supper. It will depend largely on your behaviour between now and then. Go!'

'But, father—'

Clarence dropped the paper, shaken with emotion. Mr Chugwater's sternness deepened visibly.

'Clarence! Must I speak again?'

He stooped and removed his right slipper.

Clarence withdrew.

Reggie picked up the paper.

'That kid,' he announced judicially, 'is off his nut! Hullo! I told you so! Fry not out, 104. Good old Charles!'

'I say,' exclaimed Horace, who sat nearest the window, 'there are two rummy-looking chaps coming to the front door, wearing a sort of fancy dress!'

'It must be the Germans,' said Reggie. 'The paper says they landed here this afternoon. I expect—'

A thunderous knock rang through the house. The family looked at one another. Voices were heard in the hall, and next moment the door opened and the servant announced 'Mr Prinsotto and Mr Aydycong'.

'Or, rather,' said the first of the two newcomers, a tall, bearded, soldierly man, in perfect English, 'Prince Otto of Saxe-Pfennig and Captain the Graf von Poppenheim, his aide-de-camp.'

'Just so – just so!' said Mr Chugwater, affably. 'Sit down, won't you?'

The visitors seated themselves. There was an awkward silence.

'Warm day!' said Mr Chugwater.

'Very!' said the Prince, a little constrainedly.

'Perhaps a cup of tea? Have you come far?'

'Well – er – pretty far. That is to say, a certain distance. In fact, from Germany.'

'I spent my summer holiday last year at Dresden. Capital place!'

'Just so. The fact is, Mr – er—'

'Chugwater. By the way – my wife, Mrs Chugwater.'

The Prince bowed. So did his aide-de-camp.

'The fact is, Mr Jugwater,' resumed the Prince, 'we are not here on a holiday.'

'Quite so, quite so. Business before pleasure.'

The Prince pulled at his moustache. So did his aide-de-camp, who seemed to be a man of but little initiative and conversational resource.

'We are invaders.'

'Not at all, not at all,' protested Mr Chugwater.

'I must warn you that you will resist at your peril. You wear no uniform—'

'Wouldn't dream of such a thing. Except at the lodge, of course.'

'You will be sorely tempted, no doubt. Do not think that I do not appreciate your feelings. This is an Englishman's Home.'

Mr Chugwater tapped him confidentially on the knee.

'And an uncommonly snug little place, too,' he said. 'Now, if you will forgive me for talking business, you, I gather, propose making some stay in this country.'

The Prince laughed shortly. So did his aide-de-camp. 'Exactly,' continued Mr Chugwater, 'exactly. Then you will want some *pied-à-terre*, if you follow me. I shall be delighted to let you this house on remarkably easy terms for as long as you please. Just come along into my study for a moment. We can talk it over quietly there. You see, dealing direct with me, you would escape the middleman's charges, and—'

Gently but firmly he edged the Prince out of the room and down the passage.

The aide-de-camp continued to sit staring woodenly at the carpet. Reggie closed quietly in on him.

'Excuse me,' he said; 'talking shop and all that. But I'm an agent for the Come One Come All Accident and Life Assurance Office. You have heard of it probably? We can offer you really exceptional terms. You must not miss a chance of this sort. Now here's a prospectus—'

Horace sidled forward.

'I don't know if you happen to be a cyclist, Captain – er – Graf; but if you'd like a practically new motor-bike, only been used since last November, I can let you—'

There was a swish of skirts as Grace and Alice advanced on the visitor.

'I'm sure,' said Grace winningly, 'that you're fond of the theatre, Captain Poppenheim. We are getting up a performance of "Ici on parle Français", in aid of the fund for Supplying Square Meals to Old-Age Pensioners. Such a deserving object, you know. Now, how many tickets will you take?'

'You can sell them to your friends, you know,' added Mrs Chugwater.

The aide-de-camp gulped convulsively.

Ten minutes later two penniless men groped their way, dazed, to the garden gate.

'At last,' said Prince Otto brokenly, for it was he, 'at last I begin to realise the horrors of an invasion – for the invaders.'

And together the two men staggered on.

When the papers arrived next morning, it was seen that the situation was even worse than had at first been suspected. Not only had the Germans effected a landing in Essex, but, in addition, no fewer than eight other hostile armies had, by some remarkable coincidence, hit on that identical moment for launching their long-prepared blow.

England was not merely beneath the heel of the invader. It was beneath the heels of nine invaders.

There was barely standing-room.

Full details were given in the Press. It seemed that while Germany was landing in Essex, a strong force of Russians, under the Grand Duke Vodkakoff, had occupied Yarmouth. Simultaneously the Mad Mullah had captured Portsmouth; while the Swiss navy had bombarded Lyme Regis, and landed troops immediately to westward of the bathing-machines. At precisely the same moment China, at last awakened, had swooped down upon that picturesque little Welsh watering-place, Lllgxtpll, and, despite desperate resistance on the part of an excursion of Evanses and Joneses from Cardiff, had obtained a secure foothold. While these things were happening in Wales, the army of Monaco had descended on Auchtermuchty, on the Firth of Clyde. Within two minutes of this disaster, by Greenwich time, a boisterous band of Young Turks had seized Scarborough.

And, at Brighton and Margate respectively, small but determined armies, the one of Moroccan brigands, under Raisuli, the

other of dark-skinned warriors from the distant isle of Bolly-golla, had made good their footing.

This was a very serious state of things.

Correspondents of the *Daily Mail* at the various points of attack had wired such particulars as they were able. The preliminary parley at Lllgxtpll between Prince Ping Pong Pang, the Chinese general, and Llewellyn Evans, the leader of the Cardiff excursionists, seems to have been impressive to a degree. The former had spoken throughout in pure Chinese, the latter

replying in rich Welsh, and the general effect, wired the correspondent, was almost painfully exhilarating.

So sudden had been the attacks that in very few instances was there any real resistance. The nearest approach to it appears to have been seen at Margate.

At the time of the arrival of the black warriors which, like the other onslaughts, took place between one and two o'clock on

The boyish vigour of the Young Turks.

the afternoon of August Bank Holiday, the sands were covered with happy revellers. When the war canoes approached the beach, the excursionists seem to have mistaken their occupants at first for a troupe of nigger minstrels on an unusually magnificent scale; and it was freely noised abroad in the crowd that they were being presented by Charles Frohmann, who was endeavouring to revive the ancient glories of the Christy Minstrels.

Too soon, however, it was perceived that these were no harmless Moore and Burgesses. Suspicion was aroused by the absence of banjoes and tambourines; and when the foremost of the negroes dexterously scalped a small boy, suspicion became certainty.

In this crisis the trippers of Margate behaved well. The Mounted Infantry, on donkeys, headed by Uncle Bones, did much execution. The Ladies' Tormentor Brigade harassed the enemy's flank, and a hastily-formed band of sharp-shooters, armed with three-shies-a-penny balls and milky cocos, undoubtedly troubled the advance guard considerably. But superior force told. After half an hour's brisk fighting the excursionists fled, leaving the beach to the foe.

At Auchtermuchty and Portsmouth no obstacle, apparently, was offered to the invaders. At Brighton the enemy were permitted to land unharmed. Scarborough, taken utterly aback by the boyish vigour of the Young Turks, was an easy prey; and at Yarmouth, though the Grand Duke received a nasty slap in the face from a dexterously-thrown bloater, the resistance appears to have been equally futile.

By tea-time on August the First, nine strongly-equipped forces were firmly established on British soil.

Such a state of affairs, disturbing enough in itself, was rendered still more disquieting by the fact that, except for the Boy Scouts, England's military strength at this time was practically nil.

The abolition of the regular army had been the first step. Several causes had contributed to this. In the first place, the Socialists had condemned the army system as unsocial. Privates, they pointed out, were forbidden to hob-nob with colonels, though the difference in their positions was due to a mere accident of birth. They demanded that every man in the army should be a general. Comrade Quelch, in an eloquent speech at Newington Butts, had pointed, amidst enthusiasm, to the republics of South America, where the system worked admirably.

Scotland, too, disapproved of the army, because it was professional. Mr Smith wrote several trenchant letters to Mr C. J. B. Marriott on the subject.

So the army was abolished, and the land defence of the country entrusted entirely to the Territorials, the Legion of Frontiersmen, and the Boy Scouts.

But first the Territorials dropped out. The strain of being referred to on the music-hall stage as Teddy-boys was too much for them.

Then the Frontiersmen were disbanded. They had promised

well at the start, but they had never been themselves since La Milo had been attacked by the Manchester Watch Committee. It had taken all the heart out of them.

So that in the end England's defenders were narrowed down to the Boy Scouts, of whom Clarence Chugwater was the pride, and a large civilian population, prepared, at any moment, to turn out for their country's sake and wave flags. A certain section of these, too, could sing patriotic songs.

It was inevitable, in the height of the Silly Season, that such a topic as the simultaneous invasion of Great Britain by nine foreign powers should be seized upon by the press. Countless letters poured into the offices of the London daily papers every morning. Space forbids more than the gist of a few of these.

Miss Charlesworth wrote: – 'In this crisis I see no alternative. I shall disappear.'

Mr Horatio Bottomley, in *John Bull*, said that there was some very dirty and underhand work going on, and that the secret history of the invasion would be published shortly. He himself, however, preferred any invader, even the King of Bollygolla, to some K.C.'s he could name, though he was fond of dear old Muir. He wanted to know why Inspector Drew had retired.

The *Daily Express*, in a thoughtful leader, said that Free Trade evidently meant invaders for all.

Mr Herbert Gladstone, writing to the *Times*, pointed out that he had let so many undesirable aliens into the country that he did not see that a few more made much difference.

Mr George R. Sims made eighteen puns on the names of the invading generals in the course of one number of 'Mustard and Cress'.

Mr H. G. Pélissier urged the public to look on the bright side.

There was a sun still shining in the sky. Besides, who knew that some foreign marksman might not pot the censor?

Mr Robert FitzSimmons offered to take on any of the invading generals, or all of them, and if he didn't beat them it would only be because the referee had a wife and seven small children

and had asked him as a personal favour to let himself be knocked out. He had lost several fights that way.

The directors of the Crystal Palace wrote a circular letter to the shareholders, pointing out that there was a good time coming. With this addition to the public, the Palace stood a sporting chance of once more finding itself full.

Judge Willis asked: 'What is an invasion?'

Signor Scotti cabled anxiously from America (pre-paid): 'Stands Scotland where it did?'

Mr Lewis Waller wrote heroically: 'How many of them are there? I am usually good for about half a dozen. Are they assassins? I can tackle any number of assassins.'

Mr Seymour Hicks said he hoped they would not hurt George Edwardes.

Mr George Edwardes said that if they injured Seymour Hicks in any way he would never smile again.

A writer in *Answers* pointed out that, if all the invaders in the country were piled in a heap, they would reach some of the way to the moon.

Far-seeing men took a gloomy view of the situation. They laid stress on the fact that this counter-attraction was bound to hit first-class cricket hard. For some years gates had shown a tendency to fall off, owing to the growing popularity of golf, tennis, and other games. The desire to see the invaders as they marched through the country must draw away thousands who otherwise would have paid their sixpences at the turnstiles. It was suggested that representations should be made to the invading generals with a view to inducing them to make a small charge to sightseers.

In sporting circles the chief interest centred on the race to London. The papers showed the positions of the various armies each morning in their Runners and Betting columns; six to four on the Germans was freely offered, but found no takers.

Considerable interest was displayed in the probable behaviour of the nine armies when they met. The situation was a curious outcome of the modern custom of striking a deadly blow before actually declaring war. Until the moment when the enemy were at her doors, England had imagined that she was on terms of the most satisfactory friendship with her neighbours. The foe had taken full advantage of this, and also of the fact that, owing to a fit of absent-mindedness on the part of the Government, England had no ships afloat which were not entirely obsolete. Interviewed on the subject by representatives of the daily papers, the Government handsomely admitted that it was perhaps in some ways a silly thing to have done; but, they urged, you could not think of everything. Besides, they were on the point of laying down a *Dreadnought*, which would be ready in a very few years. Meanwhile, the best thing the public could do was to sleep quietly in their beds. It was Fisher's tip; and Fisher was a smart man.

And all the while the Invaders' Marathon continued.

Who would be the first to reach London?

The Germans had got off smartly from the mark and were fully justifying the long odds laid upon them. That master-strategist, Prince Otto of Saxe-Pfennig, realising that if he wished to reach the metropolis quickly he must not go by train, had resolved almost at once to walk. Though hampered considerably by crowds of rustics who gathered, gaping, at every point in the line of march, he had made good progress. The German troops had strict orders to reply to no questions, with the result that little time was lost in idle chatter, and in a couple of days it was seen that the army of the Fatherland was bound, barring accidents, to win comfortably.

The progress of the other forces was slower. The Chinese especially had undergone great privations, having lost their way near Llanfairpwlgwnngogogoch, and having been unable to understand the voluble directions given to them by the various shepherds they encountered. It was not for nearly a week that they contrived to reach Chester, where, catching a cheap excursion, they arrived in the metropolis, hungry and footsore, four day after the last of their rivals had taken up their station.

The German advance halted on the wooded heights of Tottenham. Here a camp was pitched and trenches dug.

The march had shown how terrible invasion must of necessity be. With no wish to be ruthless, the troops of Prince Otto

With the Chinese in Wales.

had done grievous damage. Cricket-pitches had been trampled down, and in many cases even golf-greens dented by the iron heel of the invader, who rarely, if ever, replaced the divot. Everywhere they had left ruin and misery in their train.

With the other armies it was the same story. Through carefully-preserved woods they had marched, frightening the birds and driving keepers into fits of nervous prostration. Fishing, owing to their tramping carelessly through the streams, was at a standstill. Croquet had been given up in despair.

Near Epping the Russians shot a fox. . . .

The situation which faced Prince Otto was a delicate one. All his early training and education had implanted in him the fixed idea that, if he ever invaded England, he would do it either alone or with the sympathetic co-operation of allies. He had never faced the problem of what he should do if there were rivals in the field. Competition is wholesome, but only within bounds. He could not very well ask the other nations to withdraw. Nor did he feel inclined to withdraw himself.

'It all comes of this dashed Swoop of the Vulture business,' he grumbled, as he paced before his tent, ever and anon pausing to sweep the city below him with his glasses. 'I should like to find the fellow who started the idea! Making me look a fool! Still, it's just as bad for the others, thank goodness! Well, Poppenheim?'

Captain von Poppenheim approached and saluted.

'Please, sir, the men say, "May they bombard London?"'

'Bombard London!'

'Yes, sir; it's always done.'

Prince Otto pulled thoughtfully at his moustache.

'Bombard London! It seems – and yet – ah, well, they have few pleasures.'

He stood awhile in meditation. So did Captain von Poppen-heim. He kicked a pebble. So did Captain von Poppenheim – only a smaller pebble. Discipline is very strict in the German army.

'Poppenheim.'

'Sir?'

'Any signs of our – er – competitors?'

'Yes, sir; the Russians are coming up on the left flank, sir. They'll be here in a few hours. Raisuli has been arrested at Purley for stealing chickens. The army of Bollygolla is about ten miles out. No news of the field yet, sir.'

The Prince brooded. Then he spoke, unbosoming himself more freely than was his wont in conversation with his staff.

'Between you and me, Pop,' he cried impulsively, 'I'm dashed sorry we ever started this dashed silly invading business. We thought ourselves dashed smart, working in the dark, and giving no sign till the great pounce, and all that sort of dashed nonsense. Seems to me we've simply dashed well landed ourselves in the dashed soup.'

Captain von Poppenheim saluted in sympathetic silence. He and the Prince had been old chums at college. A life-long friendship existed between them. He would have liked to have expressed adhesion verbally to his superior officer's remarks. The words 'I don't think' trembled on his tongue. But the iron discipline of the German Army gagged him. He saluted again and clicked his heels.

The Prince recovered himself with a strong effort.

'You say the Russians will be here shortly?' he said.

'In a few hours, sir.'

'And the men really wish to bombard London?'

'It would be a treat to them, sir.'

'Well, well, I suppose if we don't do it, somebody else will. And we got here first.'

'Yes, sir.'

'Then—'

An orderly hurried up and saluted.

'Telegram, sir.'

Absently the Prince opened it. Then his eyes lit up.

'Götterdämmerung!' he said. 'I never thought of that. "Smash up London and provide work for unemployed mending it. – GRAYSON,"' he read. 'Poppenheim.'

'Sir?'

'Let the bombardment commence.'

'Yes, sir.'

'And let it continue till the Russians arrive. Then it must stop, or there will be complications.'

Captain von Poppenheim saluted, and withdrew.

Thus was London bombarded. Fortunately it was August, and there was nobody in town.

Otherwise there might have been loss of life.

The Russians, led by General Vodkakoff, arrived at Hampstead half an hour after the bombardment had ceased, and the rest of the invaders, including Raisuli, who had got off on an *alibi*, dropped in at intervals during the week. By the evening of Saturday, the sixth of August, even the Chinese had limped to the metropolis. And the question now was, What was going to happen? England displayed a polite indifference to the problem. We are essentially a nation of sightseers. To us the excitement of staring at the invaders was enough. Into the complex international problems to which the situation gave rise it did not occur to us to examine. When you consider that a crowd of five hundred Londoners will assemble in the space of two minutes, abandoning entirely all its other business, to watch a cab-horse that has fallen in the street, it is not surprising that the spectacle of nine separate and distinct armies in the metropolis left no room in the British mind for other reflections.

The attraction was beginning to draw people back to London now. They found that the German shells had had one excellent result: they had demolished nearly all the London statues. And what might have conceivably seemed a drawback, the fact that they had blown great holes in the wood-paving, passed unnoticed amidst the more extensive operations of the London County Council.

Taking it for all in all, the German gunners had simply been beautifying London. The Albert Hall, struck by a merciful shell, had come down with a run, and was now a heap of picturesque

ruins; Whitefield's Tabernacle was a charred mass; and the burning of the Royal Academy proved a great comfort to all. At a mass meeting in Trafalgar Square a hearty vote of thanks was passed, with acclamation, to Prince Otto.

But if Londoners rejoiced, the invaders were very far from doing so. The complicated state of foreign politics made it imperative that there should be no friction between the Powers. Yet here a great number of them were in perhaps as embarrassing a position as ever diplomatists were called upon to unravel. When nine dogs are assembled round one bone, it is rarely on the bone alone that teeth-marks are found at the close of the proceedings.

Prince Otto of Saxe-Pfennig set himself resolutely to grapple with the problem. His chance of grappling successfully with it was not improved by the stream of telegrams which arrived daily from his Imperial Master, demanding to know whether he had yet subjugated the country, and if not, why not. He had replied guardedly, stating the difficulties which lay in his way, and had received the following: 'At once mailed fist display. On Get or out Get. – WILHELM.'

It was then that the distracted Prince saw that steps must be taken at once.

Carefully-worded letters were despatched by District Messenger boys to the other generals. Towards nightfall the replies began to come in, and, having read them, the Prince saw that this business could never be settled without a personal interview. Many of the replies were absolutely incoherent.

Raisuli, apologising for delay on the ground that he had been away in the Isle of Dogs cracking a crib, wrote suggesting that the Germans and Moroccans should combine with a view to playing the Confidence Trick on the Swiss general, who seemed a simple sort of chap. 'Reminds me of dear old Maclean,' wrote Raisuli. 'There is money in this. Will you come in? Wire in the morning.'

The general of the Monaco forces thought the best way would be to settle the thing by means of a game of chance of the odd-man-out class. He knew a splendid game called Slippery Sam. He could teach them the rules in half a minute.

The reply of Prince Ping Pong Pang of China was probably brilliant and scholarly, but it was expressed in Chinese characters of the Ming period, which Prince Otto did not understand; and even if he had it would have done him no good, for he tried to read it from the top downwards instead of from the bottom up.

The Young Turks, as might have been expected, wrote in their customary flippant, cheeky style. They were full of mischief, as usual. The body of the letter, scrawled in a round, schoolboy hand, dealt principally with the details of a booby-trap which the general had successfully laid for his head of staff. 'He was frightfully shirty,' concluded the note jubilantly.

From the Bollygolla camp the messenger-boy returned without a scalp, and with a verbal message to the effect that the King could neither read nor write.

Grand Duke Vodkakoff, from the Russian lines, replied in his smooth, cynical, Russian way: – 'You appear anxious, my dear Prince, to scratch the other entrants. May I beg you to remember what happens when you scratch a Russian?'

As for the Mad Mullah's reply, it was simply pure delirium. The journey from Somaliland, and his meeting with his friend Mr Dillon, appeared to have had the worst effects on his sanity. He opened with the statement that he was a tea-pot; and that was the only really coherent remark he made.

Prince Otto placed a hand wearily on his throbbing brow.

'We must have a conference,' he said. 'It is the only way.'

Next day eight invitations to dinner went out from the German camp.

It would be idle to say that the dinner, as a dinner, was a complete success. Half-way through the Swiss general missed his diamond solitaire, and cold glances were cast at Raisuli, who sat on his immediate left. Then the King of Bollygolla's table-manners were frankly inelegant. When he wanted a thing, he grabbed for it. And he seemed to want nearly everything. Nor was the behaviour of the leader of the Young Turks all that could be desired. There had been some talk of only allowing him to come down to dessert; but he had squashed in, as he briefly put it, and it would be paltering with the truth to say that he had not had far more champagne than was good for him. Also, the general of Monaco had brought a pack of cards with him, and was spoiling the harmony by trying to induce Prince Ping Pong Pang to find the lady. And the brainless laugh of the Mad Mullah was very trying.

Altogether Prince Otto was glad when the cloth was removed, and the waiters left the company to smoke and talk business.

Anyone who has had anything to do with the higher diplomacy is aware that diplomatic language stands in a class by itself. It is a language specially designed to deceive the chance listener.

Thus when Prince Otto, turning to Grand Duke Vodkakoff, said quietly, 'I hear the crops are coming on nicely down Kent way,' the habitual frequenter of diplomatic circles would have understood, as did the Grand Duke, that what he really meant was, 'Now about this business. What do you propose to do?'

The company, with the exception of the representative of the Young Turks, who was drinking *crème de menthe* out of a tumbler, the Mullah and the King of Bollygolla bent forward, deeply interested, to catch the Russian's reply. Much would depend on this.

The great dinner party.

Vodkakoff carelessly flicked the ash off his cigarette.

'So I hear,' he said slowly. 'But in Shropshire, they tell me, they are having trouble with the mangel-wurzels.'

The Prince frowned at this typical piece of shifty Russian diplomacy.

'How is your Highness getting on with your Highness's roller-skating?' he inquired guardedly.

The Russian smiled a subtle smile.

'Poorly,' he said, 'poorly. The last time I tried the outside edge I thought somebody had thrown the building at me.'

Prince Otto flushed. He was a plain, blunt man, and he hated this beating about the bush.

'Why does a chicken cross the road?' he demanded, almost angrily.

The Russian raised his eyebrows, and smiled, but made no reply. The Prince, resolved to give him no chance of wriggling away from the point, pressed him hotly.

'Think of a number,' he cried. 'Double it. Add ten. Take away the number you first thought of. Divide it by three, and what is the result?'

There was an awed silence. Surely the Russian, expert at evasion as he was, could not parry so direct a challenge as this.

He threw away his cigarette and lit a cigar.

'I understand,' he said, with a tinkle of defiance in his voice, 'that the Suffragettes, as a last resource, propose to capture Mr Asquith and sing the Suffragette Anthem to him.'

A startled gasp ran round the table.

'Because the higher he flies, the fewer?' asked Prince Otto, with sinister calm.

'Because the higher he flies, the fewer,' said the Russian smoothly, but with the smoothness of a treacherous sea.

There was another gasp. The situation was becoming alarmingly tense.

'You are plain-spoken, your Highness,' said Prince Otto slowly.

At this moment the tension was relieved by the Young Turk falling off his chair with a crash on to the floor. Everyone jumped up startled. Raisuli took advantage of the confusion to pocket a silver ash-tray.

The interruption had a good effect. Frowns relaxed. The wranglers began to see that they had allowed their feelings to run away with them. It was with a conciliatory smile that Prince Otto, filling the Grand Duke's glass, observed:

'Trumper is perhaps the prettier bat, but I confess I admire Fry's robust driving.'

The Russian was won over. He extended his hand.

'Two down and three to play, and the red near the top corner pocket,' he said with that half-Oriental charm which he knew so well how to exhibit on occasion.

The two shook hands warmly.

And so it was settled, the Russian having, as we have seen, waived his claim to bombard London in his turn, there was no obstacle to a peaceful settlement. It was obvious that the superior forces of the Germans and Russians gave them, if they did but combine, the key to the situation. The decision they arrived at was, as set forth above, as follows. After the fashion of the moment, the Russian and German generals decided to draw the Colour Line. That meant that the troops of China, Somaliland, Bollygolla, as well as Raisuli and the Young Turks, were ruled out. They would be given a week in which to leave the country. Resistance would be useless. The combined forces of the Germans, Russians, Swiss, and Monacoans were overwhelming, especially as the Chinese had not recovered from their wanderings in Wales and were far too footsore still to think of serious fighting.

When they had left, the remaining four Powers would continue the invasion jointly.

Prince Otto of Saxe-Pfennig went to bed that night, comfortably conscious of a good work well done. He saw his way now clear before him.

But he had made one miscalculation. He had not reckoned with Clarence Chugwater.

END OF PART I

Part II. Saved!

Night!

Night in Aldwych!

In the centre of that vast tract of unreclaimed prairie known to Londoners as the Aldwych Site there shone feebly, seeming almost to emphasise the darkness and desolation of the scene, a single light.

It was the camp-fire of the Boy Scouts.

The night was raw and windy. A fine rain had been falling for some hours. The date was September the First. For just a month England had been in the grip of the invaders. The coloured section of the hostile force had either reached its home by now, or was well on its way. The public had seen it go with a certain regret. Not since the visit of the Shah had such an attractive topic of conversation been afforded them. Several comic journalists had built up a reputation and a large price per thousand words on the King of Bollygolla alone. Theatres had benefited by the influx of a large, new, unsophisticated public. A piece at the Waldorf Theatre had run for a whole fortnight, and *The Merry Widow* had taken on a new lease of life. Selfridge's, abandoning its policy of caution, had advertised to the extent of a quarter of a column in two weekly papers.

Now the Young Turks were back at school in Constantinople,

shuffling their feet and throwing ink pellets at one another; Raisuli, home again in the old mountains, was working up the kidnapping business, which had fallen off sadly in his absence under the charge of an incompetent *locum tenens*; and the Chinese, the Bollygollans, and the troops of the Mad Mullah were enduring the miseries of sea-sickness out in mid-ocean.

The Swiss army had also gone home, in order to be in time for the winter hotel season. There only remained the Germans, the Russians, and the troops of Monaco.

In the camp of the Boy Scouts a vast activity prevailed.

Few of London's millions realise how tremendous and far-reaching an association the Boy Scouts are. It will be news to the Man in the Street to learn that, with the possible exception of the Black Hand, the Scouts are perhaps the most carefully-organised secret society in the world.

Their ramifications extend through the length and breadth of England. The boys you see parading the streets with hockey-sticks are but a small section, the aristocrats of the Society. Every boy in England, and many a man, is in the pay of the association. Their funds are practically unlimited. By the oath of initiation which he takes on joining, every boy is compelled

to pay into the common coffers a percentage of his pocket-money or his salary. When you drop his weekly three-and-six-pence into the hand of your office-boy on Saturday, possibly you fancy that he takes it home to mother. He doesn't. He spends two-and-six on Woodbines. The other shilling goes into the treasury of the Boy Scouts. When you visit your nephew at Eton, and tip him five pounds or whatever it is, does he spend it at the sock-shop? Apparently, yes. In reality, a quarter reaches the common fund.

Take another case, to show the Boy Scouts' power. You are a City merchant, and, arriving at the office one morning in a bad temper, you proceed to cure yourself by taking it out of the office-boy. He says nothing, apparently does nothing. But that evening, as you are going home in the Tube, a burly working-man treads heavily on your gouty foot. In Ladbroke Grove a passing hansom splashes you with mud. Reaching home, you find that the cat has been at the cold chicken and the butler has given notice. You do not connect these things, but they are all alike the results of your unjust behaviour to your office-boy in the morning.

Or, meeting a ragged little matchseller, you pat his head and give him sixpence. Next day an anonymous present of champagne arrives at your address.

Terrible in their wrath, the Boy Scouts never forget a kindness.

The whistle of a Striped Iguanodon sounded softly in the darkness. The sentry, who was pacing to and fro before the camp-fire, halted, and peered into the night. As he peered, he uttered the plaintive note of a zebra calling to its mate.

A voice from the darkness said, 'Een gonyâma-gonyâma.'

'Invooboo,' replied the sentry argumentatively. 'Yah bô! Yah bô! Invooboo.'

An indistinct figure moved forward.

'Who goes there?'

'A friend.'

'Advance, friend, and give the countersign.'

'Remember Mafeking, and death to Injuns.'

'Pass, friend! All's well.'

The figure walked on into the firelight. The sentry started; then saluted and stood to attention. On his face was a worshipping look of admiration and awe, such as some young soldier of the Grande Armée might have worn on seeing Napoleon; for the newcomer was Clarence Chugwater.

'Your name?' said Clarence, eyeing the sturdy young warrior.

'Private William Buggins, sir.'

'You watch well, Private Buggins. England has need of such as you.'

He pinched the young Scout's ear tolerantly. The sentry flushed with pleasure.

'My orders have been carried out?' said Clarence.

'Yes, sir. The patrols are all here.'

'Enumerate them.'

'The Chinchilla Kittens, the Bongos, the Zebras, the Iguanodons, the Welsh Rabbits, the Snapping Turtles, and a half-patrol of the 33rd London Gazekas, sir.'

Clarence nodded.

''Tis well,' he said. 'What are they doing?'

'Some of them are acting a Scout's play, sir; some are doing Cone Exercises; one or two are practising deep breathing; and the rest are dancing an Old English Morris Dance.'

Clarence nodded.

'They could not be better employed. Inform them that I have arrived and would address them.'

The sentry saluted.

Standing in an attitude of deep thought, with his feet apart, his hands clasped behind him, and his chin sunk upon his breast, Clarence made a singularly impressive picture. He had left his Essex home three weeks before, on the expiration of his ten days' holiday, to return to his post of junior sub-reporter on the staff

Clarence made an impressive picture.

of a leading London evening paper. It was really only at night now that he got any time to himself. During the day his time was his paper's, and he was compelled to spend the weary hours reading off results of races and other sporting items on the tape-machine. It was only at 6 p.m. that he could begin to devote himself to the service of his country.

The Scouts had assembled now, and were standing, keen and alert, ready to do Clarence's bidding.

Clarence returned their salute moodily.

'Scout-master Wagstaff,' he said.

The Scout-master, the leader of the troop formed by the various patrols, stepped forward.

'Let the war-dance commence.'

Clarence watched the evolutions absently. His heart was ill-attuned to dances. But the thing had to be done, so it was as well to get it over. When the last movement had been completed, he raised his hand.

'Men,' he said, in his clear, penetrating alto, 'although you have not the same facilities as myself for hearing the latest news, you are all, by this time, doubtless aware that this England of ours lies 'neath the proud foot of a conqueror. It is for us to save her. (Cheers, and a voice 'Invooboo!') I would call on you here and now to seize your hockey-sticks and rush upon the invader, were it not, alas! that such an action would merely result in your destruction. At present the invader is too strong. We must wait; and something tells me that we shall not have to wait long. (Applause.) Jealousy is beginning to spring up between the Russians and the Germans. It will be our task to aggravate this feeling. With our perfect organisation this should be easy. Sooner or later this smouldering jealousy is going to burst into flame. Any day now,' he proceeded, warming as he spoke, 'there may be the dickens of a dust-up between these Johnnies, and then we've got 'em where the hair's short. See what I mean, you chaps? It's like this. Any moment they may start scrapping and chaw each other up, and then we'll simply sail in and knock what's left endways.'

A shout of applause went up from the assembled scouts.

'What I am anxious to impress upon you men,' concluded Clarence, in more measured tones, 'is that our hour approaches. England looks to us, and it is for us to see that she does not look in vain. Sedulously feeding the growing flame of animosity between the component parts of the invading horde, we may contrive to bring about actual disruption. Till that day, see to it that you prepare yourselves for war. Men, I have finished.'

'What the Chief Scout means,' said Scout-master Wagstaff, 'is no rotting about and all that sort of rot. Jolly well keep yourselves fit, and then, when the time comes, we'll give these Russian and German blighters about the biggest hiding they've ever heard of. Follow the idea? Very well, then. Mind you don't go mucking the show up.'

'Een gonyâma-gonyâma!' shouted the now thoroughly roused troops. 'Invooboo! Yah bô! Yah bô! Invooboo!'

The voice of Young England – of Young England alert and at its post!

Historians, when they come to deal with the opening years of the twentieth century, will probably call this the Music-Hall Age. At the time of the great invasion the music-halls dominated England. Every town and every suburb had its Hall, most of them more than one. The public appetite for sightseeing had to be satisfied somehow, and the music-hall provided the easiest way of doing it. The Halls formed a common place on which the celebrity and the ordinary man could meet. If an impulsive gentleman slew his grandmother with the coal-hammer, only a small portion of the public could gaze upon his pleasing features at the Old Bailey. To enable the rest to enjoy the intellectual treat, it was necessary to engage him, at enormous expense, to appear at a music-hall. There, if he happened to be acquitted, he would come on the stage, preceded by an asthmatic introducer, and beam affably at the public for ten minutes, speaking at intervals in a totally inaudible voice, and then retire; to be followed by some enterprising lady who had endeavoured, unsuccessfully, to solve the problem of living at the rate of ten thousand a year on an income of nothing, or who had performed some other similarly brainy feat.

It was not till the middle of September that anyone conceived what one would have thought the obvious idea of offering music-hall engagements to the invading generals.

The first man to think of it was Solly Quhayne, the rising young agent. Solly was the son of Abraham Cohen, an eminent agent of the Victorian era. His brothers, Abe Kern, Benjamin Colquhoun, Jack Coyne, and Barney Cowan had gravitated to the City; but Solly had carried on the old business, and was making a big name for himself. It was Solly who had met Blinky Bill Mullins, the prominent sand-bagger, as he emerged from his twenty years' retirement at Dartmoor, and booked him solid for a thirty-six months' lecturing tour on the McGinnis circuit. It was to him, too, that Joe Brown, who could eat eight pounds of raw meat in seven and a quarter minutes, owed his first chance of displaying his gifts to the wider public of the vaudeville stage.

The idea of securing the services of the invading generals came to him in a flash.

'S'elp me!' he cried. 'I believe they'd go big; put 'em on where you like.'

Solly was a man of action. Within a minute he was talking to the managing director of the Mammoth Syndicate Halls on the telephone. In five minutes the managing director had agreed to pay Prince Otto of Saxe-Pfennig five hundred pounds a week, if he could be prevailed upon to appear. In ten minutes the Grand Duke Vodkakoff had been engaged, subject to his approval, at a weekly four hundred and fifty by the Stone-Rafferty circuit. And in a quarter of an hour Solly Quhayne, having pushed his way through a mixed crowd of Tricky Serios and Versatile Comedians and Patterers who had been waiting to see him for the last hour and a half, was bowling off in a taximeter-cab to the Russian lines at Hampstead.

General Vodkakoff received his visitor civilly, but at first without enthusiasm. There were, it seemed, objections to his becoming an artiste. Would he have to wear a property bald head and sing songs about wanting people to see his girl? He didn't think he could. He had only sung once in his life, and that was twenty years ago at a bump-supper at Moscow University. And even then, he confided to Mr Quhayne, it had taken a decanter and a half of neat vodka to bring him up to the scratch.

The agent ridiculed the idea.

'Why, your Grand Grace,' he cried, 'there won't be anything of that sort. You ain't going to be starred as a *comic*. You're a Refined Lecturer and Society Monologue Artist. "How I Invaded England", with lights down and the cinematograph going. We can easily fake the pictures.'

The Grand Duke made another objection.

'I understand,' he said, 'it is etiquette for music-hall artists in their spare time to eat – er – fried fish with their fingers. Must I do that? I doubt if I could manage it.'

Mr Quhayne once more became the human semaphore.

'S'elp me! Of course you needn't! All the leading pros eat it with a spoon. Bless you, you can be the refined gentleman on the Halls same as anywhere else. Come now, your Grand Grace, is it a deal? Four hundred and fifty chinking o'Goblins a week for one hall a night, and press-agented at eight hundred and seventy-five. S'elp me! Lauder doesn't get it, not in England.'

The Grand Duke reflected. The invasion had proved more expensive than he had foreseen. The English are proverbially a nation of shopkeepers, and they had put up their prices in all the shops for his special benefit. And he was expected to do such a lot of tipping. Four hundred and fifty a week would come in uncommonly useful.

'Where do I sign?' he asked, extending his hand for the agreement.

Five minutes later Mr Quhayne was urging his taxi-driver to exceed the speed-limit in the direction of Tottenham.

Clarence read the news of the two engagements on the tape at the office of his paper, but the first intimation the general public had of it was through the medium of headlines: –

MUSIC-HALL SENSATION

INVADING GENERALS' GIGANTIC SALARIES

RUMOURED RESENTMENT OF V.A.F.

WHAT WILL WATER-RATS DO?

INTERVIEW WITH MR HARRY LAUDER

Clarence chuckled grimly as the tape clicked out the news. The end had begun. To sow jealousy between the rival generals would have been easy. To sow it between two rival music-hall artistes would be among the world's softest jobs.

Among the general public, of course, the announcement created a profound sensation. Nothing else was talked about in train and omnibus. The papers had leaders on the subject. At first the popular impression was that the generals were going to do a comedy duo act of the Who-Was-It-I-Seen-You-Coming-Down-the-Street-With? type, and there was disappointment when it was found that the engagements were for different halls. Rumours sprang up. It was said that the Grand Duke had for years been an enthusiastic amateur sword-swallower, and had, indeed, come to England mainly for the purpose of getting bookings; that the Prince had a secure reputation in Potsdam as a singer of songs in the George Robey style; that both were expert trick-cyclists.

Then the truth came out. Neither had any specialities; they would simply appear and deliver lectures.

The feeling in the music-hall world was strong. The Variety Artists' Federation debated the advisability of another strike. The Water Rats, meeting in mystic secrecy in a Maiden Lane public-house, passed fifteen resolutions in an hour and a quarter. Sir Harry Lauder, interviewed by the *Era*, gave it as his opinion that both the Grand Duke and the Prince were gowks, who would do well to haud their blether. He himself proposed to go straight to America, where genuine artists were cheered in the streets and entertained at haggis dinners, and not forced to compete with amateur sumphs and gonuphs from other countries.

Clarence, brooding over the situation like a Providence, was glad to see that already the new move had weakened the invaders'

power. The day after the announcement in the press of the approaching *début* of the other generals, the leader of the army of Monaco had hurried to the agents to secure an engagement for himself. He held out the special inducement of card-tricks, at which he was highly skilled. The agents had received him coldly. Brown and Day had asked him to call again. Foster had sent out a message regretting that he was too busy to see him.

At de Freece's he had been kept waiting in the ante-room for two hours in the midst of a bevy of Sparkling Comediennes of pronounced peroxidity and blue-chinned men in dusty bowler-hats, who told each other how they had gone with a bang at Oakham and John o' Groats, and had then gone away in despair.

On the following day, deeply offended, he had withdrawn his troops from the country.

The strength of the invaders was melting away little by little.

'How long?' murmured Clarence Chugwater, as he worked at the tape-machine. 'How long?'

It was Clarence's custom to leave the office of his newspaper at one o'clock each day, and lunch at a neighbouring Aerated Bread shop. He did this on the day following the first appearance of the two generals at their respective halls. He had brought an early edition of the paper with him, and in the intervals of dealing with his glass of milk and scone and butter, he read the report of the performances.

Both, it seemed, had met with flattering receptions, though they had appeared nervous. The Russian general especially, whose style, said the critic, was somewhat reminiscent of Mr T. E. Dunville, had made himself a great favourite with the gallery. The report concluded by calling attention once more to the fact that the salaries paid to the two – eight hundred and seventy-five pounds a week each – established a record in music-hall history on this side of the Atlantic.

Clarence had just finished this when there came to his ears the faint note of a tarantula singing to its young.

He looked up. Opposite him, at the next table, was seated a youth of fifteen, of a slightly grubby aspect. He was eyeing Clarence closely.

Clarence took off his spectacles, polished them, and replaced them on his nose. As he did so, the thin gruffle of the tarantula sounded once more. Without changing his expression, Clarence cautiously uttered the deep snarl of a sand-eel surprised while bathing.

It was sufficient. The other rose to his feet, holding his right hand on a line with his shoulder, palm to the front, thumb resting on the nail of the little finger, and the other three fingers upright.

Clarence seized his hat by the brim at the back, and moved it swiftly twice up and down.

The other, hesitating no longer, came over to his table.

'Pip-pip!' he said, in an undertone.

'Toodleoo and God save the King!' whispered Clarence.

The mystic ceremony which always takes place when two Boy Scouts meet in public was complete.

'Private Biggs of the Eighteenth Tarantulas, sir,' said the boy, respectfully, for he had recognised Clarence.

Clarence inclined his head.

'You may sit, Private Biggs,' he said graciously. 'You have news to impart?'

'News, sir, that may be of vital importance.'

'Say on.'

Private Biggs, who had brought his sparkling limado and a bath-bun with him from the other table, took a sip of the former, and embarked upon his narrative.

'I am employed, sir,' he said, 'as a sort of junior clerk and office-boy by Mr Solly Quhayne, the music-hall agent.'

Clarence tapped his brow thoughtfully; then his face cleared.

'I remember. It was he who secured the engagements of the generals.'

'The same, sir.'

'Proceed.'

The other resumed his story.

'It is my duty to sit in a sort of rabbit-hutch in the outer office, take the callers' names, and especially to see that they don't get through to Mr Quhayne till he wishes to receive them. That is the most exacting part of my day's work. You wouldn't believe how full of the purest swank some of these pros are. Tell you they've got an appointment as soon as look at you. Artful beggars!'

Clarence nodded sympathetically.

'This morning an Acrobat and Society Contortionist made such a fuss that in the end I had to take his card in to the private office. Mr Quhayne was there talking to a gentleman whom I recognised as his brother, Mr Colquhoun. They were engrossed in their conversation, and did not notice me for a moment. With no wish to play the eavesdropper, I could not help but overhear. They were talking about the generals. "Yes, I know they're press-agented at eight seventy-five, dear boy," I heard Mr Quhayne say, "but between you and me and the door-knob that isn't what they're getting. The German feller's drawing five hundred of the best, but I could only get four-fifty for the Russian. Can't say why. I should have thought, if anything, he'd be the bigger draw. Bit of a comic in his way!" And then he saw me. There was some slight unpleasantness. In fact, I've got the sack. After it was over I came away to try and find you. It seemed to me that the information might be of importance.'

Clarence's eyes gleamed.

'You have done splendidly, Private – no, *Corporal* Biggs. Do not regret your lost position. The society shall find you work. This news you have brought is of the utmost – the most vital importance. Dash it!' he cried, unbending in his enthusiasm, 'we've got 'em on the hop. If they aren't biting pieces out of each other in the next day or two, I'm jolly well mistaken.'

He rose; then sat down again.

'Corporal – no, dash it, Sergeant Biggs – you must have something with me. This is an occasion. The news you have brought me may mean the salvation of England. What would you like?'

The other saluted joyfully.

'I think I'll have another sparkling limado, thanks awfully,' he said.

The beverage arrived. They raised their glasses.

'To England,' said Clarence simply.

'To England,' echoed his subordinate.

Clarence left the shop with swift strides, and hurried, deep in thought, to the offices of the *Encore* in Wellington Street.

'Yus?' said the office-boy interrogatively.

Clarence gave the Scout's Siquand, the pass-word. The boy's demeanour changed instantly. He saluted with the utmost respect.

'I wish to see the Editor,' said Clarence.

A short speech, but one that meant salvation for the motherland.

The days following Clarence's visit to the offices of the *Encore* were marked by a growing feeling of unrest, alike among invaded and invaders. The first novelty and excitement of the foreign occupation of the country was beginning to wear off, and in its place the sturdy independence so typical of the British character was reasserting itself. Deep down in his heart the genuine Englishman has a rugged distaste for seeing his country invaded by a foreign army. People were asking themselves by what right these aliens had overrun British soil. An ever-growing feeling of annoyance had begun to lay hold of the nation.

It is probable that the departure of Sir Harry Lauder first brought home to England what this invasion might mean. The great comedian, in his manifesto in the *Times*, had not minced his words. Plainly and crisply he had stated that he was leaving the country because the music-hall stage was given over to alien gowks. He was sorry for England. He liked England. But now, all he could say was, 'God bless you.' England shuddered, remembering that last time he had said, 'God bless you till I come back.'

Ominous mutterings began to make themselves heard.

Other causes contributed to swell the discontent. A regiment of Russians, out route-marching, had walked across the bowling-screen at Kennington Oval during the Surrey v. Lancashire match, causing Hayward to be bowled for a duck's-egg. A band of German sappers had dug a trench right across the turf at Queen's Club.

The mutterings increased.

Nor were the invaders satisfied and happy. The late English

summer had set in with all its usual severity, and the Cossacks, reared in the kindlier climate of Siberia, were feeling it terribly. Colds were the rule rather than the exception in the Russian lines. The coughing of the Germans at Tottenham could be heard in Oxford Street.

The attitude of the British public, too, was getting on their nerves. They had been prepared for fierce resistance. They had pictured the invasion as a series of brisk battles – painful perhaps, but exciting. They had anticipated that when they had conquered the country they might meet with the Glare of Hatred as they patrolled the streets. The Supercilious Stare unnerved them. There is nothing so terrible to the highly-strung foreigner as the cold, contemptuous, patronising gaze of the Englishman. It gave the invaders a perpetual feeling of doing the wrong thing. They felt like men who had been found travelling in a first-class carriage with a third-class ticket. They became conscious of the size of their hands and feet. As they marched through the metropolis they felt their ears growing hot and red. Beneath the chilly stare of the populace they experienced all the sensations of a man who has come to a strange dinner-party in a tweed suit when everybody else has dressed. They felt warm and prickly.

It was dull for them, too. London is never at its best in early September, even for the *habitué*. There was nothing to do. Most of the theatres were shut. The streets were damp and dirty. It was all very well for the generals, appearing every night in the glare and glitter of the footlights; but for the rank and file the occupation of London spelt pure boredom.

London was, in fact, a human powder-magazine. And it was Clarence Chugwater who with a firm hand applied the match that was to set it in a blaze.

Clarence had called at the offices of the *Encore* on a Friday. The paper's publishing day is Thursday. The *Encore* is the *Times* of the music-hall world. It casts its curses here, bestows its benedictions (sparely) there. The *Encore* criticising the latest action of the Variety Artists' Federation is the nearest modern approach to Jove hurling the thunderbolt. Its motto is, 'Cry havoc, and let loose the performing dogs of war'.

It so happened that on the Thursday following his momentous visit to Wellington Street, there was need of someone on the staff of Clarence's evening paper to go and obtain an interview from the Russian general. Mr Hubert Wales had just published a novel so fruity in theme and treatment that it had been publicly denounced from the pulpit by no less a person than the Rev. Canon Edgar Sheppard, D.D., Sub-Dean of His Majesty's Chapels Royal, Deputy Clerk of the Closet and Sub-Almoner to the King. A morning paper had started the question, 'Should there be a Censor of Fiction?' and, in accordance with custom, editors were collecting the views of celebrities, preferably of those whose opinion on the subject was absolutely valueless.

All the other reporters being away on their duties, the editor was at a loss.

'Isn't there anybody else?' he demanded.

The chief sub-editor pondered.

'There is young blooming Chugwater,' he said.

(It was thus that England's deliverer was habitually spoken of in the office.)

'Then send him,' said the editor.

Grand Duke Vodkakoff's turn at the Magnum Palace of Varieties started every evening at ten sharp. He topped the bill. Clarence, having been detained by a review of the Scouts, did not reach the hall till five minutes to the hour. He got to the dressing-room as the general was going on to the stage.

The Grand Duke dressed in the large room with the other male turns. There were no private dressing-rooms at the Magnum. Clarence sat down on a basket-trunk belonging to the Premier Troupe of Bounding Zouaves of the Desert, and waited. The four athletic young gentlemen who composed the troupe were dressing after their turn. They took no notice of Clarence.

Presently one Zouave spoke.

'Bit off tonight, Bill. Cold house.'

'Not 'arf,' replied his colleague. 'Gave me the shivers.'

'Wonder how his nibs'll go.'

Evidently he referred to the Grand Duke.

'Oh, '*e's* all right. They eat his sort of swank. Seems to me the profession's going to the dogs, what with these bloomin' amytoors an' all. Got the 'airbrush, 'Arry?'

Harry, a tall, silent Zouave, handed over the hairbrush.

Bill continued.

'I'd like to see him go on of a Monday night at the old Mogul. They'd soon show him. It gives me the fair 'ump, it does, these toffs coming in and taking the bread out of our mouths. Why can't he give us chaps a chance? Fair makes me rasp, him and his bloomin' eight hundred and seventy-five o' goblins a week.'

'Not so much of your eight hundred and seventy-five, young feller me lad,' said the Zouave who had spoken first. 'Ain't you seen the rag this week?'

'Naow. What's in it? How does our advert look?'

'Ow, that's all right, never mind that. You look at "What the *Encore* Would Like to Know". That's what'll touch his nibs up.'

He produced a copy of the paper from the pocket of his great-coat which hung from the door, and passed it to his bounding brother.

'Read it out, old sort,' he said.

The other took it to the light and began to read slowly and cautiously, as one who is no expert at the art.

'"What the *Encore* would like to know: – Whether Prince Otto of Saxe-Pfennig didn't go particularly big at the Lobelia last week? And Whether his success hasn't compelled Agent Quhayne to purchase a larger-sized hat? And Whether it isn't a fact that, though they are press-agented at the same figure, Prince Otto is getting fifty a week more than Grand Duke Vodkakoff? And If it is not so, why a little bird has assured us that the Prince is being paid five hundred a week and the Grand Duke only four hundred and fifty? And, In any case, whether the Prince isn't worth fifty a week more than his Russian friend?" Lumme!'

An awed silence fell upon the group. To Clarence, who had dictated the matter (though the style was the editor's), the paragraph did not come as a surprise. His only feeling was one of relief that the editor had served up his material so well. He felt that he had been justified in leaving the more delicate literary work to that master-hand.

'That'll be one in the eye,' said the Zouave Harry. ''Ere, I'll stick it up opposite of him when he comes back to dress. Got a pin and a pencil, some of you?'

He marked the quarter column heavily, and pinned it up beside the looking-glass. Then he turned to his companions.

''Ow about not waiting, chaps?' he suggested. 'I shouldn't 'arf wonder, from the look of him, if he wasn't the 'aughty kind of a feller who'd cleave you to the bazooka for tuppence with his bloomin' falchion. I'm goin' to 'urry through with my dressing and wait till tomorrow night to see how he looks. No risks for Willie!'

The suggestion seemed thoughtful and good. The Bounding Zouaves, with one accord, bounded into their clothes and disappeared through the door just as a long-drawn chord from the invisible orchestra announced the conclusion of the Grand Duke's turn.

General Vodkakoff strutted into the room, listening complacently to the applause which was still going on. He had gone well. He felt pleased with himself.

It was not for a moment that he noticed Clarence.

'Ah,' he said, 'the interviewer, eh? You wish to—'

Clarence began to explain his mission. While he was doing so the Grand Duke strolled to the basin and began to remove his make-up. He favoured, when on the stage, a touch of the Raven Gipsy No. 3 grease-paint. It added a picturesque swarthiness to his appearance, and made him look more like what he felt to be the popular ideal of a Russian general.

The looking-glass hung just over the basin.

Clarence, watching him in the glass, saw him start as he read the first paragraph. A dark flush, almost rivalling the Raven Gipsy No. 3, spread over his face. He trembled with rage.

'Who put that paper there?' he roared, turning.

'With reference, then, to Mr Hubert Wales's novel,' said Clarence.

The Grand Duke cursed Mr Hubert Wales, his novel, and Clarence in one sentence.

'You may possibly,' continued Clarence, sticking to his point like a good interviewer, 'have read the trenchant, but some say justifiable remarks of the Rev. Canon Edgar Sheppard, D.D., Sub-Dean of His Majesty's Chapels Royal, Deputy Clerk of the Closet, and Sub-Almoner to the King.'

The Grand Duke swiftly added that eminent cleric to the list.

'Did you put that paper on this looking-glass?' he shouted.

'I did not put that paper on that looking-glass,' replied Clarence precisely.

'Ah,' said the Grand Duke, 'if you had, I'd have come and wrung your neck like a chicken, and scattered you to the four corners of this dressing-room.'

'I'm glad I didn't,' said Clarence.

'Have you read this paper on the looking-glass?'

'I have not read that paper on the looking-glass,' replied Clarence, whose chief fault as a conversationalist was that he was perhaps a shade too Ollendorfian. 'But I know its contents.'

'It's a lie!' roared the Grand Duke. 'An infamous lie! I've a good mind to have him up for libel. I know very well he got them to put those paragraphs in, if he didn't write them himself.'

'Professional jealousy,' said Clarence, with a sigh, 'is a very sad thing.'

'I'll professional jealousy him!'

'I hear,' said Clarence casually, 'that he *has* been going very well at the Lobelia. A friend of mine who was there last night told me he took eleven calls.'

For a moment the Russian General's face swelled apoplectically. Then he recovered himself with a tremendous effort.

'Wait!' he said, with awful calm. 'Wait till tomorrow night! I'll show him! Went very well, did he? Ha! Took eleven calls, did he? Oh, ha, ha! And he'll take them tomorrow night, too! Only' – and here his voice took on a note of fiendish purpose so terrible that, hardened scout as he was, Clarence felt his flesh creep – 'only this time they'll be cat-calls!'

And, with a shout of almost maniac laughter, the jealous artiste flung himself into a chair, and began to pull off his boots.

Clarence silently withdrew. The hour was very near.

The Grand Duke Vodkakoff was not the man to let the grass grow under his feet. He was no lobster, no flat-fish. He did it now – swift, secret, deadly – a typical Muscovite. By midnight his staff had their orders.

Those orders were for the stalls at the Lobelia.

Price of entrance to the gallery and pit was served out at day-break to the Eighth and Fifteenth Cossacks of the Don, those fierce, semi-civilised fighting-machines who know no fear.

Grand Duke Vodkakoff's preparations were ready.

Few more fortunate events have occurred in the history of English literature than the quite accidental visit of Mr Bart Kennedy to the Lobelia on that historic night. He happened to turn in there casually after dinner, and was thus enabled to see the whole thing from start to finish. At a quarter to eleven a wild-eyed man charged in at the main entrance of Carmelite House, and, too impatient to use the lift, dashed up the stairs, shouting for pens, ink and paper.

Next morning the *Daily Mail* was one riot of headlines. The whole of page five was given up to the topic. The headlines were not elusive. They flung the facts at the reader: –

SCENE AT THE LOBELIA
PRINCE OTTO OF SAXE-PFENNIG
GIVEN THE BIRD
BY
RUSSIAN SOLDIERS
WHAT WILL BE THE OUTCOME?

There were about seventeen more, and then came Mr Bart Kennedy's special report.

He wrote as follows: –

'A night to remember. A marvellous night. A night such as few will see again. A night of fear and wonder. The night of September the eleventh. Last night.

'Nine-thirty. I had dined. I had eaten my dinner. My dinner! So inextricably are the prose and romance of life blended. My dinner! I had eaten my dinner on this night. This wonderful night. This night of September the eleventh. Last night!

'I had dined at the club. A chop. A boiled potato. Mushrooms on toast. A touch of Stilton. Half-a-bottle of Beaune. I lay back in my chair. I debated within myself. A Hall? A theatre? A book in the library? That night, the night of September the eleventh, I as near as a toucher spent in the library of my club with a book. That night! The night of September the eleventh. Last night!

'Fate took me to the Lobelia. Fate! We are its toys. Its footballs. We are the footballs of Fate. Fate might have sent me to the Gaiety. Fate took me to the Lobelia. This Fate which rules us.

'I sent in my card to the manager. He let me through. Ever courteous. He let me through on my face. This manager. This genial and courteous manager.

'I was in the Lobelia. A dead-head. I was in the Lobelia as a dead-head!'

Here, in the original draft of the article, there are reflections, at some length, on the interior decorations of the Hall, and an excursus on music-hall performances in general. It is not till he

comes to examine the audience that Mr Kennedy returns to the main issue.

'And what manner of audience was it that had gathered together to view the entertainment provided by the genial and courteous manager of the Lobelia? The audience. Beyond whom there is no appeal. The Cæsars of the music-hall. The audience.'

At this point the author has a few extremely interesting and thoughtful remarks on the subject of audiences. These may be omitted.

'In the stalls I noted a solid body of Russian officers. These soldiers from the Steppes. These bearded men. These Russians. They sat silent and watchful. They applauded little. The programme left them cold. The Trick Cyclist. The Dashing Soubrette and Idol of Belgravia. The Argumentative College Chums. The Swell Comedian. The Man with the Performing Canaries. None of these could rouse them. They were waiting. Waiting. Waiting tensely. Every muscle taut. Husbanding their strength. Waiting. For what?

'A man at my side told a friend that a fellow had told him that he had been told by a commissionaire that the pit and gallery were full of Russians. Russians. Russians everywhere. Why? Were they genuine patrons of the Halls? Or were they there from some ulterior motive? There was an air of suspense. We were all waiting. Waiting. For what?

'The atmosphere is summed up in a word. One word. Sinister. The atmosphere was sinister.

'AA! A stir in the crowded house. The ruffling of the face of the sea before a storm. The Sisters Sigsbee, Coon Delineators and Unrivalled Burlesque Artists, have finished their dance, smiled, blown kisses, skipped off, skipped on again, smiled, blown more kisses, and disappeared. A long chord from the orchestra. A chord that is almost a wail. A wail of regret for that which is past. Two liveried menials appear. They carry sheets of cardboard. These menials carry sheets of cardboard. But not blank sheets. On each sheet is a number.

'The number 15.

'Who is number 15?

'Prince Otto of Saxe-Pfennig. Prince Otto, General of the German Army. Prince Otto is Number 15.

'A burst of applause from the house. But not from the Russians. They are silent. They are waiting. For what?

'The orchestra plays a lively air. The massive curtains part. A tall, handsome military figure strides on to the stage. He bows. This tall, handsome, military man bows. He is Prince Otto of Saxe-Pfennig, General of the Army of Germany. One of our conquerors.

'He begins to speak. "Ladies and Gentlemen." This man, this general, says, "Ladies and Gentlemen."

'But no more. No more. No more. Nothing more. No more. He says, "Ladies and Gentlemen," but no more.

'And why does he say no more? Has he finished his turn? Is that all he does? Are his eight hundred and seventy-five pounds a week paid him for saying, "Ladies and Gentlemen"?

'No!

'He would say more. He has more to say. This is only the beginning. This tall, handsome man has all his music still within him.

'Why, then, does he say no more? Why does he say "Ladies and Gentlemen", but no more? No more. Only that. No more. Nothing more. No more.

'Because from the stalls a solid, vast, crushing "Boo!" is hurled at him. From the Russians in the stalls comes this vast, crushing "Boo!" It is for this that they have been waiting. It is for this that they have been waiting so tensely. For this. They have been waiting for this colossal "Boo!"

'The General retreats a step. He is amazed. Startled. Perhaps frightened. He waves his hands.

'From gallery and pit comes a hideous whistling and howling.

The noise of wild beasts. The noise of exploding boilers. The noise of a music-hall audience giving a performer the bird.

'Everyone is standing on his feet. Some on mine. Everyone is shouting. This vast audience is shouting.

'Words begin to emerge from the babel.

'"Get offski! Rotten turnovitch!" These bearded Russians, these stern critics, shout, "Rotten turnovitch!"

'Fire shoots from the eyes of the German. This strong man's eyes.

'"Get offski! Swankietoff! Rotten turnovitch!"

'The fury of this audience is terrible. This audience. This last court of appeal. This audience in its fury is terrible.

'What will happen? The German stands his ground. This man of blood and iron stands his ground. He means to go on. This strong man. He means to go on if it snows.

'The audience is pulling up the benches. A tomato shatters itself on the Prince's right eye. An over-ripe tomato.

'"Get offski!" Three eggs and a cat sail through the air. Falling short, they drop on to the orchestra. These eggs! This cat! They fall on the conductor and the second trombone. They fall like the gentle dew from Heaven upon the place beneath. That cat! Those eggs!

'AA! At last the stage-manager – keen, alert, resourceful – saves the situation. This man. This stage-manager. This man with the big brain. Slowly, inevitably, the fireproof curtain falls. It is half-way down. It is down. Before it, the audience. The audience. Behind it, the Prince. The Prince. That general. That man of iron. That performer who has just got the bird.

'The Russian National Anthem rings through the hall. Thunderous! Triumphant! The Russian National Anthem. A pæan of joy.

'Get offski! Rotten turnovitch!'

'The menials reappear. Those calm, passionless menials. They remove the number fifteen. They insert the number sixteen. They are like Destiny – Pitiless, Unmoved, Purposeful, Silent. Those menials.

'A crash from the orchestra. Turn number sixteen has begun...'

Prince Otto of Saxe-Pfennig stood in the wings, shaking in every limb. German oaths of indescribable vigour poured from his lips. In a group some feet away stood six muscular, short-sleeved stage-hands. It was they who had flung themselves on the general at the fall of the iron curtain and prevented him dashing round to attack the stalls with his sabre. At a sign from the stage-manager they were ready to do it again.

The stage-manager was endeavouring to administer balm.

'Bless you, your Highness,' he was saying, 'it's nothing. It's what happens to everyone some time. Ask any of the top-notch pros. Ask 'em whether they never got the bird when they were starting. Why, even now some of the biggest stars can't go to some towns because they always cop it there. Bless you, it—'

A stage-hand came up with a piece of paper in his hand.

'Young feller in spectacles and a rum sort o' suit give me this for your 'Ighness.'

The Prince snatched it from his hand.

The note was written in a round, boyish hand. It was signed, 'A Friend'. It ran: – 'The men who booed you tonight were sent for that purpose by General Vodkakoff, who is jealous of you because of the paragraphs in the *Encore* this week.'

Prince Otto became suddenly calm.

'Excuse me, your Highness,' said the stage-manager anxiously, as he moved, 'you can't go round to the front. Stand by, Bill.'

'Right, sir!' said the stage-hands.

Prince Otto smiled pleasantly.

'There is no danger. I do not intend to go to the front. I am going to look in at the Scotch Stores for a moment.'

'Oh, in that case, your Highness, good-night, your Highness! Better luck tomorrow, your Highness!'

It had been the custom of the two generals, since they had joined the music-hall profession, to go, after their turn, to the Scotch Stores, where they stood talking and blocking the gangway, as etiquette demands that a successful artiste shall.

The Prince had little doubt but that he would find Vodkakoff there tonight.

He was right. The Russian general was there, chatting affably across the counter about the weather.

He nodded at the Prince with a well-assumed carelessness.

'Go well tonight?' he inquired casually.

Prince Otto clenched his fists; but he had had a rigorously diplomatic up-bringing, and knew how to keep a hold on himself. When he spoke it was in the familiar language of diplomacy.

'The rain has stopped,' he said, 'but the pavements are still wet underfoot. Has your grace taken the precaution to come out in a good stout pair of boots?'

The shaft plainly went home, but the Grand Duke's manner, as he replied, was unruffled.

'Rain,' he said, sipping his vermouth, 'is always wet; but sometimes it is cold as well.'

'But it never falls upwards,' said the Prince, pointedly.

'Rarely, I understand. Your powers of observation are keen, my dear Prince.'

There was a silence; then the Prince, momentarily baffled, returned to the attack.

'The quickest way to get from Charing Cross to Hammersmith Broadway,' he said, 'is to go by Underground.'

'Men have died in Hammersmith Broadway,' replied the Grand Duke suavely.

The Prince gritted his teeth. He was no match for his slippery adversary in a diplomatic dialogue, and he knew it.

'The sun rises in the East,' he cried, half-choking, 'but it sets – it sets!'

'So does a hen,' was the cynical reply.

The last remnants of the Prince's self-control were slipping away. This elusive, diplomatic conversation is a terrible strain if one is not in the mood for it. Its proper setting is the gay, glittering ball-room at some frivolous court. To a man who has just got the bird at a music-hall, and who is trying to induce another man to confess that the thing was his doing, it is little short of maddening.

'Hen!' he echoed, clenching and unclenching his fists. 'Have you studied the habits of hens?'

The truth seemed very near to him now, but the master-diplomat before him was used to extracting himself from awkward corners.

'Pullets with a southern exposure,' he drawled, 'have yellow legs and ripen quickest.'

The Prince was nonplussed. He had no answer.

The girl behind the bar spoke.

'You do talk silly, you two!' she said.

It was enough. Trivial as the remark was, it was the last straw. The Prince brought his fist down with a crash on the counter.

'Yes,' he shouted, 'you are right. We do talk silly; but we shall do so no longer. I am tired of this verbal fencing. A plain answer to a plain question. Did you or did you not send your troops to give me the bird tonight?'

'My dear Prince!'

The Grand Duke raised his eyebrows.

'Did you or did you not?'

'The wise man,' said the Russian, still determined on evasion, 'never takes sides, unless they are sides of bacon.'

The Prince smashed a glass.

'You did!' he roared. 'I know you did! Listen to me! I'll give you one chance. I'll give you and your precious soldiers twenty-four hours from midnight tonight to leave this country. If you are still here then—'

He paused dramatically.

The Grand Duke slowly drained his vermouth.

'Have you seen my professional advertisement in the *Era*, my dear Prince?' he asked.

'I have. What of it?'

'You noticed nothing about it?'

'I did not.'

'Ah. If you had looked more closely, you would have seen the words, "Permanent address, Hampstead".'

'You mean—?'

'I mean that I see no occasion to alter that advertisement in any way.'

There was another tense silence. The two men looked hard at each other.

'That is your final decision?' said the German.

The Russian bowed.

'So be it,' said the Prince, turning to the door. 'I have the honour to wish you a very good night.'

'The same to you,' said the Grand Duke. 'Mind the step.'

The news that an open rupture had occurred between the Generals of the two invading armies was not slow in circulating. The early editions of the evening papers were full of it. A symposium of the opinions of Dr Emil Reich, Dr Saleeby, Sandow, Mr Chiozza Money, and Lady Grove was hastily collected. Young men with knobbly and bulging foreheads were turned on by their editors to write character-sketches of the two generals. All was stir and activity.

Meanwhile, those who look after London's public amusements were busy with telephone and telegraph. The quarrel had taken place on Friday night. It was probable that, unless steps were taken, the battle would begin early on Saturday. Which, it did not require a man of unusual intelligence to see, would mean a heavy financial loss to those who supplied London with its Saturday afternoon amusements. The matinées would suffer. The battle might not affect the stalls and dress-circle, perhaps, but there could be no possible doubt that the pit and gallery receipts would fall off terribly. To the public which supports the pit and gallery of a theatre there is an irresistible attraction about a fight on anything like a large scale. When one considers that a quite ordinary street-fight will attract hundreds of spectators, it will be plainly seen that no theatrical entertainment could hope to compete against so strong a counter-attraction as a battle between the German and Russian armies.

The various football-grounds would be heavily hit, too. And there was to be a monster roller-skating carnival at Olympia. That also would be spoiled.

A deputation of amusement-caterers hurried to the two camps within an hour of the appearance of the first evening paper. They put their case plainly and well. The Generals were obviously impressed. Messages passed and repassed between the two armies, and in the end it was decided to put off the outbreak of hostilities till Monday morning.

Satisfactory as this undoubtedly was for the theatre-managers and directors of football clubs, it was in some ways a pity. From the standpoint of the historian it spoiled the whole affair. But for the postponement, readers of this history might – nay, would – have been able to absorb a vivid and masterly account of the great struggle, with a careful description of the tactics by which victory was achieved. They would have been told the disposition of the various regiments, the stratagems, the dashing advances, the skilful retreats, and the Lessons of the War.

As it is, owing to the mistaken good-nature of the rival generals, the date of the fixture was changed, and practically all that a historian can do is to record the result.

A slight mist had risen as early as four o'clock on Saturday. By night-fall the atmosphere was a little dense, but the lamp-posts were still clearly visible at a distance of some feet, and nobody, accustomed to living in London, would have noticed anything much out of the common. It was not till Sunday morning that the fog proper really began.

London awoke on Sunday to find the world blanketed in the

densest, yellowest London particular that had been experienced for years. It was the sort of day when the City clerk has the exhilarating certainty that at last he has an excuse for lateness which cannot possibly be received with harsh disbelief. People spent the day indoors and hoped it would clear up by tomorrow.

'They can't possibly fight if it's like this,' they told each other.

But on the Monday morning the fog was, if possible, denser. It wrapped London about as with a garment. People shook their heads.

'They'll have to put it off,' they were saying, when all of a sudden – *Boom!* And, again, *Boom!*

It was the sound of heavy guns.

The battle had begun!

One does not wish to grumble or make a fuss, but still it does seem a little hard that a battle of such importance, a battle so outstanding in the history of the world, should have been fought under such conditions. London at that moment was richer than ever before in descriptive reporters. It was the age of descriptive reporters, of vivid pen-pictures. In every newspaper office there were men who could have hauled up their slacks about that battle in a way that would have made a Y.M.C.A. lecturer want to get at somebody with a bayonet; men who could have handed out the adjectives and exclamation-marks till you almost heard the roar of the guns. And there they were – idle, supine – like careened battleships. They were helpless. Bart Kennedy did start an article which began, 'Fog. Black fog. And the roar of guns. Two nations fighting in the fog,' but it never came to anything. It was promising for a while, but it died of inanition in the middle of the second stick.

It was hard.

The lot of the actual war-correspondents was still worse. It was useless for them to explain that the fog was too thick to give them a chance. 'If it's light enough for them to fight,' said their editors remorselessly, 'it's light enough for you to watch them.' And out they had to go.

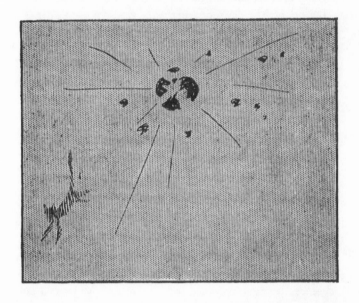

They had a perfectly miserable time. Edgar Wallace seems to have lost his way almost at once. He was found two days later in an almost starving condition at Steeple Bumpstead. How he got there nobody knows. He said he had set out to walk to where the noise of the guns seemed to be, and had gone on walking. Bennett Burleigh, that crafty old campaigner, had the sagacity to go by Tube. This brought him to Hampstead, the scene, it turned out later, of the fiercest operations, and with any luck he might have had a story to tell. But the lift stuck half-way up, owing to a German shell bursting in its neighbourhood, and it was not till the following evening that a search-party heard and rescued him.

The rest – A. G. Hales, Frederick Villiers, Charles Hands, and the others – met, on a smaller scale, the same fate as Edgar Wallace. Hales, starting for Tottenham, arrived in Croydon, very tired, with a nail in his boot. Villiers, equally unlucky, fetched up at Richmond. The most curious fate of all was reserved for Charles Hands. As far as can be gathered, he got on all right till he reached Leicester Square. There he lost his bearings, and seems to have walked round and round Shakespeare's statue, under the impression that he was going straight to Tottenham. After a day and a half of this he sat down to rest, and was there found, when the fog had cleared, by a passing policeman.

And all the while the unseen guns boomed and thundered, and strange, thin shoutings came faintly through the darkness.

It was the afternoon of Wednesday, September the Sixteenth. The battle had been over for twenty-four hours. The fog had thinned to a light lemon colour. It was raining.

By now the country was in possession of the main facts. Full details were not to be expected, though it is to the credit of the newspapers that, with keen enterprise, they had at once set to work to invent them, and on the whole had not done badly.

Broadly, the facts were that the Russian army, out-manœuvred, had been practically annihilated. Of the vast force which had entered England with the other invaders there remained but a handful. These, the Grand Duke Vodkakoff among them, were prisoners in the German lines at Tottenham.

The victory had not been gained bloodlessly. Not a fifth of the German army remained. It is estimated that quite two-thirds of each army must have perished in that last charge of the Germans up the Hampstead heights, which ended in the storming of Jack Straw's Castle and the capture of the Russian general.

Prince Otto of Saxe-Pfennig lay sleeping in his tent at Totten-ham. He was worn out. In addition to the strain of the battle, there had been the heavy work of seeing the interviewers, signing autograph-books, sitting to photographers, writing testimonials for patent medicines, and the thousand and one other tasks, burdensome but unavoidable, of the man who is in the public eye. Also he had caught a bad cold during the battle. A bottle of ammoniated quinine lay on the table beside him now as he slept.

As he lay there the flap of the tent was pulled softly aside. Two figures entered. Each was dressed in a flat-brimmed hat, a coloured handkerchief, a flannel shirt, football shorts, stockings, brown boots, and a whistle. Each carried a hockey-stick. One, however, wore spectacles and a look of quiet command which showed that he was the leader.

They stood looking at the prostrate general for some moments. Then the spectacled leader spoke.

'Scout-Master Wagstaff.'

The other saluted.

'Wake him!'

Scout-Master Wagstaff walked to the side of the bed, and shook the sleeper's shoulder. The Prince grunted, and rolled over on to his other side. The Scout-Master shook him again. He sat up, blinking.

As his eyes fell on the quiet, stern, spectacled figure, he leaped from the bed.

'What – what – what,' he stammered. 'What's the beadig of this?'

He sneezed as he spoke, and, turning to the table, poured out and drained a bumper of ammoniated quinine.

'I told the sedtry pardicularly not to let adybody id. Who are you?'

The intruder smiled quietly.

'My name is Clarence Chugwater,' he said simply.

'Jugwater? Dod't doe you frob Adab. What do you want?

If you're forb sub paper, I cad't see you now. Cub toborrow bordig.'

'I am from no paper.'

'Thed you're wud of these photographers. I tell you, I cad't see you.'

'I am no photographer.'

'Thed what are you?'

The other drew himself up.

'I am England,' he said with a sublime gesture.

'Igglud! How do you bead you're Igglud? Talk seds.'

Clarence silenced him with a frown.

'I say I am England. I am the Chief Scout, and the Scouts are England. Prince Otto, you thought this England of ours lay prone and helpless. You were wrong. The Boy Scouts were watching and waiting. And now their time has come. Scout-Master Wagstaff, do your duty.'

The Scout-Master moved forward. The Prince, bounding to the bed, thrust his hand under the pillow. Clarence's voice rang out like a trumpet.

'Cover that man!'

The Prince looked up. Two feet away Scout-Master Wagstaff was standing, catapult in hand, ready to shoot.

'He is never known to miss,' said Clarence warningly.

The Prince wavered.

'He has broken more windows than any other boy of his age in South London.'

The Prince sullenly withdrew his hand – empty.

'Well, whad do you wad?' he snarled.

'Resistance is useless,' said Clarence. 'The moment I have plotted and planned for has come. Your troops, worn out with fighting, mere shadows of themselves, have fallen an easy prey. An hour ago your camp was silently surrounded by patrols of Boy Scouts, armed with catapults and hockey-sticks. One rush and the battle was over. Your entire army, like yourself, are prisoners.'

'The diggids they are!' said the Prince blankly.

'England, my England!' cried Clarence, his face shining with a holy patriotism. 'England, thou art free! Thou hast risen from the ashes of thy dead self. Let the nations learn from this that it is when apparently crushed that the Briton is to more than ever be feared.'

'Thad's bad grabbar,' said the Prince critically.

'It isn't,' said Clarence with warmth.

'It *is*, I tell you. Id's a spud idfididive.'

Clarence's eyes flashed fire.

'I don't want any of your beastly cheek,' he said. 'Scout-Master Wagstaff, remove your prisoner.'

'All the sabe,' said the Prince, 'id *is* a splid idfididive.'

Clarence pointed silently to the door.

'And you doe id is,' persisted the Prince. 'And id's spoiled your big sbeech. Id—'

'Come on, can't you,' interrupted Scout-Master Wagstaff.

'I *ab* cubbing, aren't I? I was odly sayig—'

'I'll give you such a whack over the shin with this hockey-stick in a minute!' said the Scout-Master warningly. 'Come *on!*'

The Prince went.

The brilliantly-lighted auditorium of the Palace Theatre.

Everywhere a murmur and stir. The orchestra is playing a selection. In the stalls fair women and brave men converse in excited whispers. One catches sentences here and there.

'Quite a boy, I believe!'

'How perfectly sweet!'

''Pon honour, Lady Gussie, I couldn't say. Bertie Bertison, of the Bachelors', says a feller told him it was a clear thousand.'

'Do you hear that? Mr Bertison says that this boy is getting a thousand a week.'

'Why, that's more than either of those horrid generals got.'

'It's a lot of money, isn't it?'

'Of course, he did save the country, didn't he?'

'You may depend they wouldn't give it him if he wasn't worth it.'

'Met him last night at the Duchess's hop. Seems a decent little chap. No side and that, if you know what I mean. Hullo, there's his number!'

The orchestra stops. The number 7 is displayed. A burst of applause, swelling into a roar as the curtain rises.

A stout man in crinkled evening-dress walks on to the stage.

'Ladies and Gentlemen,' he says, 'I 'ave the 'onour tonight

Clarence at the Duchess's.

to introduce to you one whose name is, as the saying goes, a nouse'old word. It is thanks to 'im, to this 'ero whom I 'ave the 'onour to introduce to you tonight, that our beloved England no longer writhes beneath the ruthless 'eel of the alien oppressor. It was this 'ero's genius – and, I may say – er – I may say genius – that, unaided, 'it upon the only way for removing the cruel conqueror from our beloved 'earths and 'omes. It was this 'ero

who, 'aving first allowed the invaders to claw each other to 'ash (if I may be permitted the expression) after the well-known precedent of the Kilkenny cats, thereupon firmly and without flinching, stepped bravely in with his fellow-'eroes – need I say I allude to our gallant Boy Scouts? – and dexterously gave what-for in no uncertain manner to the few survivors who remained.'

Here the orator bowed, and took advantage of the applause to replenish his stock of breath. When his face had begun to lose the purple tinge, he raised his hand.

'I 'ave only to add,' he resumed, 'that this 'ero is engaged exclusively by the management of the Palace Theatre of Varieties, at a figure previously undreamed of in the annals of the music-hall stage. He is in receipt of the magnificent weekly salary of no less than one thousand one 'undred and fifty pounds a week.'

Thunderous applause.

'I 'ave little more to add. This 'ero will first perform a few of those physical exercises which have made our Boy Scouts what they are, such as deep breathing, twisting the right leg firmly round the neck, and hopping on one foot across the stage. He will then give an exhibition of the various calls and cries of the Boy Scouts – all, as you doubtless know, skilful imitations of real living animals. In this connection I 'ave to assure you that he 'as nothing whatsoever in 'is mouth, as it 'as been sometimes suggested. In conclusion he will deliver a short address on the subject of 'is great exploits. Ladies and gentlemen, I have finished, and it only now remains for me to retire, 'aving duly announced to you England's Darling Son, the Country's 'Ero, the Nation's Proudest Possession – Clarence Chugwater.'

A moment's breathless suspense, a crash from the orchestra, and the audience are standing on their seats, cheering, shouting, stamping.

A small, sturdy, spectacled figure is on the stage.

It is Clarence, the Boy of Destiny.

THE END

The Military Invasion of America

A Remarkable Tale of the German–Japanese Invasion in 1916

It may be thought that in this story Mr Wodehouse has painted in too lurid colors the horrors of a foreign invasion of the United States. Realism, it may be argued, can be carried too far. We prefer to think that our readers will acquit the author of a desire to rouse America to a sense of peril, and only by setting down without flinching the results of an invasion can this be done. If *McClure's* and all the other magazines can do it, why shouldn't *Vanity Fair* have a shot at it? Mr Wodehouse holds an established position as a military expert, his two recent articles, 'What to Do When the Zeppelin Comes,' and 'Is It Contrary to International Law for Germany to Use Culture as a Weapon of Offense,' having caused widespread comment and alarm among military students everywhere.

CHAPTER 1

The invasion of America was complete. The navy, its morale completely sapped by grape-juice, had offered but slight resistance to the German Armada: and the army, too proud to fight, had stood around, while the Japanese established their foothold on the soil of God's Own Country.

Once begun, it had proceeded apace. New York had been bombarded, – but fortunately, as it was summer, nobody of any importance was in town. Philadelphia, though ably defended by military correspondents of the *Saturday Evening Post*, had fallen at last. America was beneath the heel of the invader, whose only casualties consisted of a detachment of infantry who had been rash enough to travel on the New York, New Haven and Hartford Railroad – with the usual results.

Far-seeing patriots took a gloomy view of this state of affairs. For some years the receipts of baseball had been falling off, and it was argued that this counter-attraction must hit the national sport hard. The desire to see the invaders as they marched through the country must inevitably draw away thousands who would otherwise have paid their half-dollars to sit in the bleachers.

By the end of August, a powerful army of Germans under Prince Otto of Saxe-Pfennig had established itself at Kew Gardens, while an equally powerful horde of Japanese under General Owoki was in possession of Yonkers and all points west.

This was a very serious state of things.

CHAPTER 2

It has been well said that the crisis always produces the man, or necessity is the mother of the man, or something like that: and never has this admirable truth (of which I regret that I cannot remember the exact wording) been better exemplified than in this hour of America's sorest straits.

At a moment when everything seemed blackest, along came Clarence Chugwater.

Today the name of Clarence Chugwater is familiar to all. Everyone has seen the Chugwater Column in Central Park, the equestrian statue in Chugwater Avenue (formerly Broadway), and the Chugwater picture-postcards in the shop-windows. But at the time of the great invasion Clarence was practically unknown except in the newspaper office where he was employed as an office-boy. And even there he was not known by name. The staff habitually addressed him as Young Bone-Head.

Today, it is hard to understand how even a City editor (notoriously one of the least intelligent of human beings) could have failed to detect in the lad's face the promise of future greatness. That bulging forehead, distended with useful information (for Clarence attended night-school); those eyes, gleaming behind their tortoise-shell-rimmed spectacles; that massive chin; that *tout ensemble*; that *je ne sais quoi*.

* * *

Why, if the City editor had had a grain of sense, he would have flooded New York with electric signs, bearing the legend:

DO YOU KNOW THAT
CLARENCE CHUGWATER
IS WITH
THE *SENTINEL*?

Instead of which, he called him Bone-Head, and often with shocking adjectives prefixed. What a world!

Clarence Chugwater, that many-sided boy, was not only a prop of the *Daily Sentinel*, he was the Pride of the Boy Scouts. When off duty, he might be seen walking abroad, dressed neatly but not gaudily, in a flat-brimmed hat, a flannel shirt, a bunch of ribbons, a knapsack, knickerbockers, brown shoes, a whistle, and a long stick. He could do everything that the Boy Scout must learn to do. He could low like a bull. He could gurgle like a wood-pigeon. He could imitate the cry of the turnip in order to deceive rabbits. He could spoor, fell trees (unless their owner saw him at it), tell the character by the sole of the shoe, and fling the squaler. He did all these things well, but what he was best at was flinging the squaler.

America's defenders at this time were practically limited to the Boy Scouts and to a large civilian population, prepared at any moment to turn out for their country's sake and wave flags. A certain section of these, too, could sing patriotic songs. It would have been well, then, had the Invaders, before making too sure that America lay beneath their heel, stopped to reckon with Clarence Chugwater.

But did they? Not by a jug-full. They had never even heard of Clarence.

What was to be the result of this over-confidence?

Ah!

CHAPTER 3

It was inevitable that at a time like August, when there is never anything very much going on, such a topic as the simultaneous invasion of America by Germany and Japan should be seized upon by the press. Few of the papers failed to give the matter several columns of space, and the public found the fascination of staring at the invading troops a pleasant change from the garish attractions of South Beach and Coney Island. When you consider that a crowd of five hundred New Yorkers will assemble in the space of two minutes, abandoning entirely all its other business, to watch a man putting a new tire on his automobile, it is not surprising that the interest taken in the invaders was somewhat general.

A piquancy was added to the situation by the fact that the Germans and Japanese were not acting in any way as allies. What had happened was a curious outcome of the modern custom of striking a deadly blow before actually declaring war. By a mere chance it had occurred independently to both the Kaiser and the Mikado that it would not be half a bad idea to invade America and they had done it. The position of the Prince Saxe-Pfennig and General Owoki was consequently delicate in the extreme.

* * *

All Prince Otto's early training and education had implanted in him the fixed idea that, if he ever invaded America, he would do it either alone or with the sympathetic cooperation of allies. He had never faced the problem of what he should do if there were rivals in the field. He could not very well ask the Japanese to withdraw, and, if he withdrew himself, that meant a *mauvais quart d'heure* with the Kaiser when he got back to Germany.

'It all comes of this "Swoop of the Vulture" business,' he grumbled to General von Poppenheim, his chief of staff, 'this silly business of invading a country before you declare war on it. I suppose there's nothing for it,' said the Prince, 'but to have a talk with Owoki. Get him on the 'phone, Pop, and ask him to lunch with us at the Ritz tomorrow, to talk things over.'

The momentous conversation took place, accordingly, on the following day. It was conducted in the language of diplomacy, which, as anyone who has seen this year's crop of war plays is aware, stands in a class by itself. It is a language specially designed to deceive the chance listener.

Thus, when the Prince, turning to Owoki, as the latter consumed his portion of buckwheat cakes and maple syrup, said 'I hear the crops are coming on nicely down Tokio way,' none of the waiters perceived anything remarkable in the words. But Owoki, nursed from the cradle in an atmosphere of diplomatic subtlety, understood at once that what the Prince meant was 'Now, about this business of America. What do you propose to do about it?'

Owoki hesitated for a moment, then replied blandly: 'The food here is good, but I am not sure that I do not prefer the Honble Childs.'

The Prince frowned at this typical piece of shifty Oriental diplomacy.

'How are you getting along with your fox trotting?' he inquired guardedly.

The Japanese general smiled a subtle smile.

'Poorly,' he said, 'poorly. The last time I tried it, I thought somebody had thrown honble building at me.'

Prince Otto flushed. He was a plain, blunt man, and he hated this beating about the bush.

But what could he do? His Imperial Master would not wish him, save in the direst extremity, to fight the Japanese. Perhaps he had better yield the point. It was with a conciliatory smile, then, that, having ordered a second cup of coffee, he observed:

'Speaking of Mrs Vernon Castle, I hear that she's in again.'

And then the two shook hands.

And so it was settled, the Japanese general having, as we have seen, waived his claim to bombard New York in his turn, and the Prince having withdrawn his demand for a season pass to the Polo Grounds. There was now no obstacle in the way of an alliance.

Prince Otto went to bed that night conscious of good work well done. He now saw his way clear before him.

But he had made one miscalculation. He had omitted to reckon with Clarence Breamworthy Chugwater, the Boy Scout.

CHAPTER 4

N<small>ight!</small>

Night in Gramercy Park!

In the center of that vast tract of unreclaimed park there shone feebly, seeming almost to emphasize the darkness and desolation of the scene, a single light.

It was the camp-fire of the Boy Scouts.

The night was raw and windy. A fine rain had been falling for some hours. The date was October the First. In the camp of the Boy Scouts a vast activity prevailed.

Few of Manhattan's teeming millions realize how tremendous and far-reaching an organization the Boy Scouts are. With the possible exception of the Black Hand and the war-correspondents of the *Saturday Evening Post*, the Scouts are perhaps the most carefully-organized secret society in the world.

The power of the Scouts is enormous. Let us suppose that you are a business-man, and, arriving at the office one morning in a bad temper, you cure yourself by taking it out of the office-boy. He says nothing; he apparently does nothing. But that evening, as you enter your train for Forest Hills, a burly artisan treads on your gouty toe. Reaching home, you find that the chickens have been at your early peas, the cat has stolen the fish, and the cook has jumped her job. You do not connect these things, but they are all alike the results of your unjust behavior to Little Scout-master Cyril in the morning.

Or, meeting a ragged newsboy, you pat his head, give him a dime, and ask him if he means to be President when he grows up. Next day an anonymous present of champagne arrives at your address.

Terrible in their wrath, the Boy Scouts never forget a kindness.

A whistle sounded softly in the darkness. The sentry, pacing to and fro before the camp-fire, halted and peered into the night.

'Who goes there?'

'A friend.'

'Advance, friend: give the countersign.'

'Death to Germany and Japan.'

'Pass, friend! All's well.'

An indistinct figure walked into the firelight. The sentry started, then stood at attention. The newcomer was Clarence Chugwater.

'Your name?' said Clarence, eyeing the sturdy young warrior.

'Private William Buggins.'

'You watch well, Private Buggins. America has need of such as you.'

Clarence pinched the young Scout's ear tolerantly. The boy flushed with pleasure.

'My orders have been carried out? The patrols are here?'

'Yes, sir.'

'Enumerate them.'

Standing in an attitude of deep thought, with his feet apart, his hands clasped behind him, and his chin sunk upon his breast, Clarence made a strangely impressive picture. The Scouts hearing of his arrival were charging desperately in all directions, at last they assembled, and were soon standing, alert and attentive. Clarence returned their salute moodily. He raised his hand.

'Men,' he said, in his clear, penetrating alto, 'you are all aware by this time that our country has been invaded. It is for us to crush the invader. (Cheers, and a voice "You said it!") I would call on you here and now to seize your sticks and rush upon the alien intruders, but at present their forces are too strong. We must wait. And something tells me that we shall not have to wait long. (Applause.) Soon jealousy must inevitably spring up between the Germans and the Japanese. It will be our task to aggravate that feeling. Sooner or later this smouldering jealousy will burst into flames, and then will come our time. See that it finds you ready. I have finished.'

'Chugwater, Chugwater, Rah! Rah! Rah!' shouted the now thoroughly aroused troops.

It was the voice of Young America – of Young America alert, desperate, and at its post!

CHAPTER 5

Historians, when they come to deal with the opening years of the Twentieth Century, will probably call this the Vaudeville Age. At this time the vaudeville-halls dominate America. At the time of our story, the public appetite for sight-seeing had to be satisfied somehow, and the vaudeville-house provided the best solution. If, for example, an impulsive gentleman slew his wife and children with the ice-pick, only a small portion of the public could gaze upon his pleasing features during the trial. But when he had been acquitted under the Unwritten Law, it was necessary, to enable the great public to enjoy this intellectual treat, to engage him, at enormous expense, to appear in Vaudeville.

It was not till the middle of October, 1916, that anyone conceived what one would have thought the obvious idea of offering vaudeville engagements to the invading generals, Prince Otto, and General Owoki.

The first man to think of it was Solly Quhayne, the rising young vaudeville agent. Solly was the son of Abraham Cohen, an eminent agent of the later nineteenth century. His brothers, Abe Kern, Benjamin Colquhoun, Jack Coyne, and Barney Cowan, had gravitated to the curb market, but Solly had carried on his father's vaudeville business, and was making a big name for himself.

The idea of securing Prince Otto and General Owoki for his theatres came to him in a flash!

Solly was a man of action. Within a minute he was talking to the managing director of the Keith circuit, on the telephone. In five minutes the managing director had agreed to pay Prince Otto of Saxe-Pfennig twenty-five hundred dollars a week. In ten minutes the Japanese general had been engaged by the Orpheum Circuit at a weekly salary of two thousand dollars. And in a quarter of an hour Solly Quhayne, having pushed his way through the crowd in his ante-room, was bowling off in a taxi to the Japanese lines, at Yonkers.

General Owoki received his visitor civilly, but at first without enthusiasm. It seemed that he was shy about becoming an artist. Would he have to wear a property bald head and sing rag-time? He didn't think he could. He had only sung once in his life, and that was twenty years ago, at a class reunion at Tokio.

'Why, general,' said Solly, 'it won't be anything of that sort. You ain't going to be head-lined as a *comic*. You're a Refined Lecturer and Society Monolog Artist. "How I Invaded America," with lights down and the cinematograph going. Is it a deal?'

Two thousand dollars would come in uncommonly useful.

'Where do I sign?' the general said, extending his hand for the contract.

Five minutes later, Solly Quhayne was exceeding the speed limit in the direction of the German encampment.

Clarence Chugwater read the news of the two vaudeville engagements on the tape at the office of the *Sentinel*, a newspaper where he worked as an office-boy. He chuckled grimly. To sow jealousy between two rival vaudeville headliners should be easy.

Among the general public the announcement created a profound sensation. At first the popular impression was that the generals were going to do a comedy-duo act of the Who-Was-It-I-Seen-You-Coming-Down-The-Street-With? type, and there was disappointment when it was found that the engagements were for different houses. Rumors sprang up. It was said that General Owoki had for years been an enthusiastic amateur buck-and-wing dancer, and had, indeed, come to America mainly for the purpose of securing bookings: that Prince Otto had a secure reputation in Berlin as a singer of the Al Jolson type: that both were expert trick-cyclists.

Then the truth came out. Neither had any specialties: they would simply appear and deliver monologs.

It was Clarence Chugwater's custom to leave the office of his newspaper at one o'clock each day and lunch at a neighboring Codington's. As he sipped his milk, he read the newspaper reports of the appearances in vaudeville of the two generals. According to the paper, each was drawing a salary of five thousand dollars a week.

Clarence had just finished reading the reports when he looked up and saw, standing before him, a boy of about fifteen years.

After a moment or two the boy saluted.

'Private Biggs of the Eighteenth, sir,' he said. 'I have information.'

'Say on, Private Biggs,' said Clarence.

'I am employed, sir, as a sort of office-boy and junior clerk by Solly Quhayne, the vaudeville agent, the man who secured the engagements of the invading generals. This morning, happening to pass Mr Quhayne's room, I overheard him talking to his brother, Mr Colquhoun. They were talking about the generals.

"Yes, I know they are press-agented at five thousand a week," Mr Quhayne was saying, "but between you and me that isn't what they are getting. The German's pulling down twenty-five hundred, and the Jap gets two thousand. Can't say why he gets less. I should have thought he was a better draw. He's a good comic, in his way."'

Clarence's eyes gleamed.

'Magnificent, Private – no, *Sergeant* Biggs. You have given me valuable information.'

He raised his glass.

'To America!'

'To America!' echoed his subordinate.

Deep in thought, Clarence hurried to the offices of the *Encore*, the vaudeville weekly.

CHAPTER 6

The days following Clarence's visit to the offices of the *Encore* were marked by a growing feeling of unrest. The first novelty of the foreign occupation of the country was beginning to wear off, and the sturdy independence of the American character was reasserting itself. Deep down in his heart the genuine American has a rugged distaste for seeing his country invaded by a foreign army. People were asking themselves by what right these aliens had overrun American soil. An ever-growing feeling of annoyance had begun to lay hold of the nation. New York had become a human powder-magazine, and it was Clarence Chugwater who, with a firm hand, applied the match that was to set it in a blaze.

The *Encore* is published on Thursdays. It so happened that on the Thursday following his momentous call at the office, there was need of someone on the staff of the *Sentinel*, Clarence's paper, to go and obtain an interview with the Japanese general. Clarence's editor was at a loss. Finally he had an inspiration.

'Send young bone-head Chugwater,' he said.

(It was thus that America's deliverer was spoken of in the *Sentinel* office!)

General Owoki's act at the Palace Theatre started every evening at ten sharp. Clarence, having been detained by a review of the Boy Scouts, arrived as the general was going on the stage, and waited in the dressing-room. Presently a long-drawn chord from the invisible orchestra announced the conclusion of the act, and the general returned, obviously in high good humor.

'You went well?', inquired Clarence respectfully.

'I was honble riot,' responded the general affably.

'You are so popular,' said Clarence, 'that it seems extraordinary to me – and I think I may say that I speak for the whole of the vaudeville public – that you should be receiving five hundred dollars a week less than Prince Otto of Saxe-Pfennig.'

Not all the traditions of the Samurai could prevent the general from starting and uttering an exclamation.

'What!'

'It is in this paper,' said Clarence, producing the *Encore*. 'Let me read it to you. It is headed "What the *Encore* Would Like to Know," and it runs as follows: "Whether Prince Otto of Saxe-Pfennig did not go particularly big at the Colonial last week? And whether it is not a fact that, though they are press-agented at the same figure, his Nibs of the Fatherland is not drawing down five hundred cold iron men more than the Jap? And whether, seeing the way he goes, the Prince isn't worth twice that much more than the Japanese lemon?"'

A hoarse cry interrupted him.

'It says that?'

'I have read it verbatim. It strikes me as most unjust. Prince Otto is not worth more than you, general.'

'I believe that honble German boob wrote distinguished paragraph himself!'

'Very possibly. Professional jealousy is a sad thing. Though,' went on Clarence, 'I believe the Prince *is* going very big. They tell me that last night he took eleven calls.'

General Owoki pulled himself together with a supreme effort.

'Tomorrow night,' he said between his teeth, 'he will take more than that. But they will be honble cat-calls!'

Accounts vary so much as to what exactly did take place at the Colonial Theatre on the following night that it is hard to get at the exact truth. All eye-witnesses, however, are agreed that, just as Prince Otto of Saxe-Pfennig strode upon the stage and said 'Ladeez 'n gemmen, with your kind indulgence—', there arose from every part of the house such a storm of disapproval that he was unable to continue. From floor to roof the building was packed with Japanese soldiers, and shouts of 'Get off honble stage!' 'Procure distinguished hook!' and the like, rendered it impossible for the Prince to proceed. Finally the stage-manager dropped the curtain, to the accompaniment of the Japanese National Anthem, thunderously delivered.

It had been the custom of the two generals, since joining the vaudeville profession, to proceed after their act to a neighboring saloon, where they would stand talking about themselves and blocking up the gangway, as etiquette demands that a successful artist shall. The Prince, leaving the Colonial, after his disastrous fiasco, had no doubt that he would find the man responsible for his downfall there.

He was right. The Japanese general was at the bar, chatting affably to the bar-keeper. He nodded at the Prince with well-assumed carelessness.

'Knock 'em tonight?' he inquired casually.

Prince Otto clenched his fists.

'Look here,' he said, 'did you or did you not send your soldiers to give me the bird tonight? You did! I know you did! Well, I'll give you and your precious soldiers one chance, – twenty-four hours from midnight to leave this country. If you are still here then—'

General Owoki slowly drained his high-ball.

'Have you seen my professional advertisement in the *Dramatic Mirror*, Prince? It says "Permanent Address, General Delivery, Yonkers." You get my distinguished meaning, Stephen?'

'You mean—?'

'I mean that I see no occasion to alter that advertisement in any way. I beg to wish you honble goodnight.'

The great battle was over. I have not considered it necessary to describe it, from the first shot to the final capitulation of the practically annihilated Japanese, for that has been done more ably than I can do it by Senator Beveridge, Richard Harding Davis, Corra Harris, Mary Roberts Rinehart, Ernest Poole, Perceval Gibbon, Robert Dunn, John Reed, Irvin Cobb, and every other able-bodied American citizen with the price of a typewriter.

The German victory had not been gained bloodlessly. It was but a shattered wreck of an army that remained after the final charge up the wooded steeps of Yonkers....

Prince Otto of Saxe-Pfennig lay sleeping in his tent. He was worn out. In addition to the strain of the battle, which had taken place in perfectly beastly weather, there had been the heavy work of seeing the interviewers, signing autograph-books for school-girls, sitting to photographers, signing contracts for the moving-pictures, writing testimonials for patent medicines and Tuxedo tobacco, and the thousand and one tasks, burdensome but unavoidable, of the man who is in the public eye. Also he had caught a bad cold during the battle. A bottle of quinine was on the table beside him.

As he lay there, the flap of the tent was pulled softly aside. Two figures entered. Each was dressed in the regulation costume of the Boy Scout. One, however, wore tortoise-shell-rimmed spectacles and an air of quiet superiority which showed that he was the leader.

'Corporal Wagstaff,' he said, 'wake him.'

The boy shook the sleeper's shoulder. The Prince sat up, blinking.

'What – what – what is the beadig of this?' he stammered. 'I told the sedtry particularly not to let adybody in. If you're frob sub paper, call toborrow. I cadt see you.'

The spectacled leader drew himself up.

'I am America,' he said with a sublime gesture.

'Aberica? How do you bead you're Aberica?'

Clarence – for it was he – continued, with a frown.

'I say I am America. I am the Chief Scout, and the Boy Scouts are America. Prince Otto, you thought our country lay prone and helpless. You are wrong. The Boy Scouts were watching and waiting. And now their time has come. Corporal Wagstaff, do your duty.'

The Prince looked up. Two feet away, Corporal Wagstaff was standing, with a toy sling in hand, ready to shoot.

'Well, whad do you want?' he snarled.

'Resistance is useless,' said Clarence. 'The moment for which I have plotted has arrived. Your troops, worn with fighting, are mere shadows of their former selves. They have fallen an easy prey. An hour ago your camp was silently surrounded by Boy Scouts. One rush and the battle was over. Your entire army – like yourself – are prisoners.'

'The diggids they are!' said the Prince blankly.

'America, my America!' cried Clarence, his face shining with a holy patriotism. 'America, thou art free! Let the nations learn from this that it is when apparently crushed that America is to more than ever be feared!'

'That's bad grabbar,' said the Prince critically.

Clarence's eyes flashed fire.

'I don't want you getting fresh with me,' he said. 'Corporal Wagstaff, remove your prisoner.'

'All the sabe,' said the Prince, 'it *is* bad grabbar. It's a split infinitive, and it's spoiled your big speech.'

Clarence pointed silently to the door.

'Come on, can't you,' said Corporal Wagstaff.

'I *ab* cubbing, aren't I? I was odly sayig—'

'I'll give you such a whack over the shin in a minute,' said Corporal Wagstaff warningly. 'Come *on!*' The Prince went.

The brilliantly lighted auditorium of the Colonial Theatre.

Everywhere a murmur and a stir.

In the seats fair women and brave men converse in excited whispers. One catches sentences here and there.

'Quite a boy, I believe!'

'I've heard he's getting $10,000 a week!'

'Why, that's more than either of those horrid generals ever got!'

'It's a lot of money. But then, of course, he did save our country.'

The orchestra stops. The number 7 is displayed. A burst of applause, swelling into a roar as the curtain rises.

A stout man in crinkled evening-dress walks on the stage.

'Ladies and gentlemen, I have the honor to present to you tonight one whose name is, as the saying is, a household word. It was this hero's genius, and I may say – er – genius, that, unaided, hit upon the only way of removing the cruel conqueror from our beloved hearths and homes. It was this hero who, having first permitted the invaders to claw themselves into hash, after the well-known precedent of the Kilkenny cats, thereupon firmly and without flinching stepped in with his brave Boy Scouts and gave them what was coming to them. I have only to add that this hero has been engaged exclusively by the Colonial Palace of Varieties at a figure previously undreamed-of in the annals of the vaudeville stage. I have little to add. This hero will first perform a few physical exercises which have made the Boy Scouts what they are. He will low like a bull. He will gurgle like a wood-pigeon. He will spoor, tell the character by the sole of the shoe, and fling the squaler. He will then give imitations of very real living animals. In this connection I have to assure you that he has nothing whatsoever in his mouth, as it has some-times been suggested. Before uttering the cries, he will gargle in full view of the audience, thus rendering deception impossible. Ladies and gentlemen, it only remains for me to introduce to you America's Darling Son, the Nation's Hero, our champion and proudest possession, – Clarence Chugwater.'

A moment's breathless suspense, a crash from the orchestra, and the audience are standing on their seats, cheering, and shouting.

A small, sturdy, tortoise-shell-spectacled figure is on the stage. It is Clarence, the Boy of Destiny.

THE END

TITLES IN THE EVERYMAN WODEHOUSE

This edition of P. G. Wodehouse has been prepared from the first British printing of each title.

The Everyman Wodehouse is printed on acid-free paper and set in Caslon, a typeface designed and engraved by William Caslon of William Caslon & Son, Letter-Founders in London around 1740.